THE MAGICAL MAN OF MIRTH

Marie Wood
118 Deluare ave
Pennegrove
N J

TO THEIR GREAT JOY, THE HOT SPRING WAS AT LAST FOUND

The Magical Man of Mirth

TEXT BY

ELBRIDGE H. SABIN

PICTURES BY

ELENORE PLAISTED ABBOTT

AND

HELEN ALDEN KNIPE

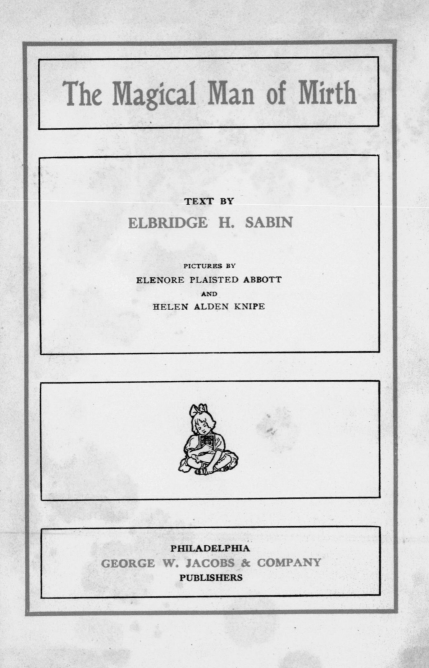

PHILADELPHIA

GEORGE W. JACOBS & COMPANY

PUBLISHERS

CONTENTS

ILLUSTRATIONS

CHAPTER I
ALL ABOARD

The Magical Man of Mirth

CHAPTER I

ALL ABOARD

In a certain town, perhaps not very far from where you yourself live, stands a big white house with green blinds, red chimneys, and a high roof crowned with brass lightning-rods. The surrounding lawn, broad and smooth, extends as far behind the building as it does in front. Thus is formed a glorious back-yard, which, because quiet and concealed from prying eyes, makes a grand playground. So thinks Dollie Lane, the little girl who dwells in the big white house, and so would you think should you visit her.

On the summer evening when this story opens, Dollie was sitting in her swing that hangs beneath a mighty tree of oak, whose gnarled and knotted branches reach from the porch almost to the barn. In her lap lay her slate which she always carries back and forth from school, and on which she had intended doing sums for the morrow's lesson. However, under the spell of the beautiful twilight, she had put off her work, and, with her eyes turned towards the eastern sky, was idly dreaming.

A slight thunder-storm had just passed by. Enough rain had fallen to freshen the air and to wash the dusty face of every tired leaf and blade. Now, with rumblings that each moment grew fainter, the massive clouds were vanishing into the east—all except one huge fellow who dallied behind as though loath to leave.

"What a monster he is!" cried Dollie, who, in common with other little girls, has the habit of talking to herself when alone. "He must be 'most a mile thick. My! but he's white and fluffy in the middle, like one of mamma's soda-biscuits. P'raps he looks more like a great splash of lather on some giant's blue shaving-mug. Wish I could go up there and sit on him, and let my legs hang over. Maybe inside of him is the home of the fairies and I could see one of them. Don't you want to go, too, Miss Martha?"

This last question was addressed to her beloved slate, of which she made a constant companion, and to which she had given the name of Miss Martha. "When do you think we shall start?" she continued. "Needn't tell me you don't know the way. You know everything. First you were papa's; then brother Bob's; then sister Mary's; and now you're mine. I 'xpect a billion lessons have been written on you and rubbed into you, and teacher says when things are rubbed into us we don't ever forget 'em. Then you're the wisest woman in all the world."

As she talked, without thinking she picked up her pencil, and half way between the middle and the top of the slate she drew a horizontal line. Then from one end of the line to the other she traced a slight curve.

No sooner had she so done than a soft voice, from out her lap, wherein lay the slate, thus addressed her: "Well, I'm indeed glad you've given me a mouth at last. It's ages and ages since I've been able to talk. But while you're about it, you might as well furnish me a nose so I can breathe better, and a couple of eyes and ears. Please, that's a dear."

"I'm not much of a drawer," replied Dollie, all excited, "but I'll do the best I can."

Quickly she placed a little triangle right above the curved line, for a nose; two tiny circles, O O near the upper corners, for eyes; and below them, for ears, two funny curlicues.

When all this was completed Miss Martha, for it was she who had spoken, seemed to feel better. "Thank you very much," she said. "Now I can use all my senses. How sweet the air smells after the shower; what a bright, neat child you are; and what is that queer noise up in the tree-top?"

Dollie listened, but could hear nothing. "Guess it was only the wind," she answered. "The wind's always zipping and swishing 'round. You'll get used to it after a while. Now tell me, is your name really Miss Martha, and do you know everything?"

"That name will do as well as any other; but

I can't claim to be such a very wise person. Perhaps I'm half the wisest person in the world, or the wisest person in half the world, or—, oh, dear, what do I want to say?"

"Never mind now," replied Dollie. "You're just as sweet and modest as you can be. You 'mind me of my old Aunt Nancy, who always wears a black silk gown, with such beaut'ful white lace 'round the throat. P'raps some day I'll make you a lace cap like hers."

Here again came an outburst of noise from the top of the old oak-tree, this time so loud that Dollie herself was disturbed.

"Whatever does make all that racket?" she inquired. "Must be our cat Ebenezer. He's awful rude, but you needn't mind him."

"I certainly shall tell him what I think of him when he comes down," remarked Miss Martha. "As I was saying, I have learned a great deal, for I've been carried three times from primary to high school; but you'll soon be through with me. All the children buy those silly tablets these days, and you'll follow the fashion."

"I shan't either," contradicted Dollie, stoutly;

"I'll use you always, p'raps even when I'm big 'nough to go to college. But I s'pose some day I'll stop studying. Wonder to who you'll go then. There aren't any more children in our fam'ly."

"Remember your grammar," cautioned Miss Martha. "You should say 'to whom,' not 'to who.'"

Now the rumpus in the tree-top broke forth once more, and a voice, loud and shrill as a blast from a horn, shouted, "To who! to who!! to who-o-o!!!"

This rather startled Dollie, but Miss Martha appeared not the least bit confused.

"I don't care who owns that voice or what owns that voice. 'To whom' is correct, and 'to who' is incorrect," she insisted.

"To who! to who!" again issued from the tree, but this time from the lower branches. Then,— flip, flap, flop, thud,—something struck the ground; and, lo and behold, in front of Dollie there stood a gigantic owl, so tall that his head was higher than hers as she sat in the swing.

Fixing his yellow, unwinking eyes on the girl

LO AND BEHOLD! IN FRONT OF DOLLY THERE STOOD A GIGANTIC OWL

and her friend, the monster commenced to speak, without waiting for an introduction.

"To who!" cried he. "I am Sir Oliver Owl, the wisest being in all the world. What do you and Miss Slate know but books? Bah! I also know the great world outside. Look at my big eyes and think of all they have seen. Look at my sharp ears and think of all they have heard. Look at my broad wings, and think into what strange places they have carried me. I can tell you why the stem of a flower grows up, and the roots grow down; I have seen the pot of gold at the end of the rainbow; I visit the people of the clouds and converse with them. One may read many books and still be a fool. I alone am wise."

After he had delivered this speech, Sir Owl began to strut back and forth, with all the pomp and dignity of a prize peacock on parade. Dollie was about to laugh at his silly antics, when suddenly he began to talk again.

"You were mentioning grammar just before I came down. Let me try you on addition. How much is who plus who?"

"Why, you can't add words," giggled Dollie, and even Miss Martha uttered a faint chuckle.

"Don't tell me that," answered Sir Owl, gruffly. "Only last Friday, after your teacher had made you a nice talk, I heard her ask one of the visitors to come up on the platform and *add a few words* to what she had said. You should remember. Listen; who plus who equals two who. The answer I told you before I asked the question. Are you any better on multiplication? How much is four feet times five quarts?"

"But you can't——" commenced Dollie again, until stopped by Miss Martha, who nudged her vigorously.

"You must humor him, my dear," whispered she. "I do believe he's crazy. The thing to do is to agree with him."

"I'm afraid I can't answer that, either," admitted Dollie, after this warning. "But let's don't play school any more. There's 'nough of that daytimes. Let's all do something."

"And what shall we do?" asked Sir Owl, much mollified now that he had shown off his superior wisdom. "If I can be of any service to you and to Miss Slate, as escort or otherwise, pray command me."

"I say let's go somewhere, don't you, Miss Martha? I've never been anywhere 'cept out to Uncle Tom's farm and once to the state fair."

"I'm perfectly wild to visit strange countries," agreed Miss Martha. "I'll go wherever you will, provided Sir Owl will conduct us."

"Since you've been on earth all your lives," suggested he, "I should think you'd like to travel in the air. Suppose we explore the big cloud Dollie saw at sunset. What do you say to that?"

"Oh, goody!" cried Dollie. "That would be magnif'cent. But could you go so high and so far?"

"Easy as scat. Why, once without stopping I flew from quarter of north to half-past south and wasn't tired at all. One of my brothers flew from the bottom of down to the top of up, where it was so hot all his feathers singed off and he fell to the earth and was killed. I'm stronger than he was. You sit on my back and hold Miss Slate in your lap. I'll take you there safe and sound. It's not very far away."

"B'lieve I better do as Miss Martha says," concluded Dollie, after a moment's thought. "She's older than I am. But p'raps I ought to ask mamma."

"She's so busy telling a caller about her new bonnet that she won't miss you. It's too good a chance to lose," exclaimed Miss Martha. "We might start at once, if Sir Owl is ready."

Sir Owl was ready. Stepping forward he bent down his head and spread out his wings, showing a broad back covered with feathers, soft as a pillow. Taking Miss Martha in her arms, Dollie quickly seated herself most comfortably. She found that she could hold on securely by thrusting each foot under one of the wings, close to the body.

"All a-b-o-a-r-d!" shouted Sir Owl. "All ready!" answered Dollie and Miss Martha; and away they went.

"To who! To who-o-o-o!!" tooted the bird, as, a few feet above the pavement, he steered his course along the street that led towards the east. In the darkness the yellow light from his two big eyes streamed out ahead like the glare from an automobile. The regular flapping of his wings sounded like the puffing of a gasoline engine.

Alarmed by what appeared to be an approaching motor, boys and girls at play in the road scurried to the curbing and perched themselves there to watch the monster dash by; a fat policeman shouted a warning to halt, and, until he was left behind, panted after them in a desperate effort to learn the number of the offending machine; while a street car, approaching around a corner, was brought to a stop so suddenly that passengers were thrown from their seats.

All this amused Dollie and Miss Martha greatly, but Sir Oliver attended strictly to the business of the moment. Slowly but surely his pinions smote the air with increasing speed; slowly but surely he rose higher and higher. Above the fences, the trees, the houses, the factory chimneys, he soared. Finally, the city was left behind; the earth seemed to drop far below; and Dollie, awed by the powerful rush of her conveyance, imagined herself on some mighty airship instead of the back of a bird.

With a little yawn of content, she first made sure that Miss Martha was in a safe place in her lap. Then she leaned her head against Sir Owl's tail, and before she knew it she was fast asleep.

CHAPTER II
THE CITY OF MIRTH

CHAPTER II

THE CITY OF MIRTH

When Dollie awoke the sun was peeping above the horizon as though he really did not know whether to get up or go back to bed. However, the sight of Sir Owl and his strange burden must have aroused his curiosity, for immediately he bounded into full view, prepared to stay for the remainder of the day.

One glance assured Dollie that everything was all right. The owl's wings were beating the air vigorously and steadily as at the beginning of the trip, and Miss Martha looked as snug and comfortable as could be. True, there was not a cloud in sight, but Dollie remembered that often they reappear shortly after a clear sunrise.

"You feel pretty good this morning, Miss Martha?" she asked, pleasantly.

"No, I do not," was the petulant reply. "I didn't sleep all night, not one single, solitary wink. What if you should drop me? I'd break into ten thousand pieces. And what do we know about this old bird, anyway? It's my opinion he's eloped with me and has stolen you; and he'll never take us back—never, never."

"There, there," murmured Dollie, soothingly. "You're all nervous. Trav'ling makes your head dizzy and achy, as it does my mamma's. Want me to bathe your face? 'Scuse me, and I'll fix myself first."

Attached by a string to one corner of the slate was a clean, new sponge, which had been dampened by the dew. With this Dollie washed her face and hands, and dried them on her handkerchief. Then she treated Miss Slate in the same manner, being careful not to rub out any of the lines she had drawn the evening before.

"Well, that *is* better," admitted Miss Martha. "But see how the ground is rising. If we don't look out it'll hit us."

"We're going to 'light," shouted Dollie. "You sit still in my lap so you won't get broken if we bump."

On motionless wings Sir Owl dipped lower and lower; then, in gradually decreasing circles, round and round he sailed in search of a good spot whereon to descend. One moment Dollie saw beneath her a green field, watered by a tiny brook; the next, a vast group of trees, brilliantly colored like gigantic flowers. It was on the edge of the field, close to the trees, that Sir Owl finally settled, gently as a falling leaf.

"My, but I'm glad to have something solid under me again," chirped Miss Slate, as Dollie laid her on the grass, that she herself might have a better opportunity to stretch her own arms and legs. "I think you've lost your way, Mr. Owl. If that's true, you must own up. There's nothing I hate more than to be deceived."

"I lose my way!" snorted the owl, in fine disdain; "I, who know all the air paths and all the air currents! Through the entire night, without one pause or break, I have flown straight towards the cloud we seek. The trouble is, a wind from the west has blown the cloud away as fast as I have approached; but I'll reach it in the end. I'm the wisest being in the world, and I never give in nor give up."

"But why did you stop?" asked Dollie. "Are

you all tuckered out with flying so far?"

"No, indeed," retorted Sir Owl. "All my race are strong, and I'm the strongest of my race. I never tire, and I never flag. But my eyes, so useful in the darkness, are dazzled and dazed by the sun. So here must we remain until twilight. You and Miss Slate amuse yourselves as you please. I shall roost in a nearby tree and meditate."

This exactly suited Dollie, who was anxious to explore the wonderful forest; so, tucking Miss Martha under one arm, she set out, while Sir Owl called after her: "Perhaps you can find a chestnut horse tree. Don't think it's quite time for horses to be ripe, but you might pick a pony to play with."

"A chestnut horse tree; pick a pony!" repeated Dollie. "Why, Sir Owl's tongue is all tangled up. He must be half asleep and dreaming of horse chestnuts."

"Don't you be too sure," cautioned Miss Martha. "For my part, I believe this whole place is enchanted, and there's no telling what we may find. Have you ever seen such funny colored woods before in all your life?"

Dollie was sure she had not. The silver birch was really silver, and shone like a polished coffee pot on Sunday morning. The yellow pine was truly golden, and glistened in the sunlight as does a gilded cross on a church steeple. The red cedar seemed to be clad in a scarlet golfing-jacket; and here and there a bunch of somber black oaks served as a background for their more showy companions. Dollie wandered around in a perfect ecstasy of delight, and even Miss Martha forgot her troubles and was glad she had come.

Soon a peculiar tree attracted attention. "Look at that," cried Dollie; "there's one all covered with footballs. I'm going to pick some and take them home to Bob."

"I should say they're cocoanuts," declared Miss Martha. "If so, you might have break-fast."

Dollie thought this a good idea. As she drew nearer she noticed that a steam with a most appetizing odor was escaping through two or three holes in the top of each of the many brown globes with which the tree was laden. Cautiously she touched the one nearest her. As it was not too warm to handle she picked it and removed the cover with which it was provided. To her joy the inside was filled with thick chocolate, seasoned precisely to suit her taste, while in the top was a piece of cocoanut cake and two cocoanut wafers. Cake for breakfast was a trifle unusual, but this was no time to be particular; so she made a hearty meal. Then the two friends strolled on to see what would be found next.

Soon Miss Martha exclaimed, "Don't you hear horses neighing and stamping? Sounds to me like a whole livery stable."

"B'lieve I do," answered Dollie; "let's hurry and see."

Hastening as fast as she could, she reached the edge of a round glade, carpeted with velvety grass, and occupied by only one tree, which grew in its center. There was nothing strange about this, but both Dollie and Miss Martha shouted in astonishment when they saw that a dozen or more chestnut ponies were fastened to the ends of the lower branches. Here indeed was a chestnut horse tree.

Each animal was prancing and dancing as though anxious for some one to ride him; nor was it resented when Dollie came up and patted one after another on· the head and neck. There was no danger that they would escape, because the branches were attached to their shoulders so firmly that Dollie, try as she might, could not break them off.

"Well, they're not ripe 'nough to pick, that's sure," she announced; "but here's one with a nice saddle. I'm going to sit on his back."

She mounted easily, and, as a matter of habit, shouted, "Get up," just as soon as she had smoothed down her skirts. Imagine her surprise at what followed. At once every pony, including her own, commenced to trot round and round in a circle. This they could do because the branches grew out from a heavy wooden ring which slipped about the trunk like the hub of a wheel around the axle.

"It's a live merry-go-round," cried she, "and you don't have to pay any nickel, either. We can ride forever and ever for nothing. Isn't that great, Miss Martha?"

And she did ride, if not forever and ever, at least until thoroughly tired out. Then she slipped from her steed, who stopped at her command, laid Miss Martha on the turf, and stretched herself out beside her for a nap.

It was a strange noise that aroused them from their slumbers. At first both feared some prowling beast, because the long shadows showed that night was coming on. However, as soon as they had collected their scattered senses, they smiled at their alarm, for the noise was the call of Sir Owl.

"To who! to who!" rang the blast from his horn, at regular intervals. "We're coming; we're coming!" yelled Dollie in reply, as, with Miss Martha in her arms, she dashed through the dusky woods, in the direction of the sound.

They found the owl upon the ground. He was stamping up and down impatiently, and the glare from his eyes proved that he was ready for departure.

"Hurry and climb up," he commanded, as soon as he saw them. "The wind has changed, and is bringing the cloud back. We can reach it in a few moments and save time. All a-b-o-a-r-d!"

Quick as a wink, Dollie and Miss Martha took their places, and, quick as a wink, the owl commenced his flight. When once more above the tree-tops, Dollie could plainly see, almost directly over them, a huge cloud shaped exactly like the one she had beheld from the swing; but this was black, while the first had been white, except when tinted pink by the setting sun.

As the floating mass came closer, she discovered that it was composed of a great many layers, like slabs of black marble, with rough and overlapping ends, piled one above the other. Between the layers were numerous tunnels or passages, the mouths of which gleamed dully, as if poorly lighted by smoky lamps. Half way between top and bottom a projecting ledge offered a safe landing. Here Sir Oliver settled, with as little ceremony as though returning to his own home; then, flapping his wings and stretching up his neck, he sent ringing down the corridor his familiar challenge. "To who! to who!"

In response to this summons there approached

a little old man, no taller than Dollie. His face and hands were pallid white, but his hair and all his clothes were jet black. He appeared worn and weary, and, as he shuffled towards the visitors, he leaned heavily on his cane.

"Who are you?" he asked, in a quavering voice, "and why come you here? Know you not that I am warder of this portal? At present no one may enter. This is the command of the Queen of the City of Mirth. If you are friendly callers, depart in peace; but if you are allies of the Magical Man of Mirth, beware lest you be made to suffer for the misdeeds of that base monster."

"Softly, softly, my venerable warder," replied Sir Owl. "We are friends who know nothing of this man of whom you speak. Truly it seems that some dire calamity has befallen this fair cloud. I am Sir Oliver Owl, the wisest being in all the universe. Miss Slate and Dollie, my companions, are not lacking in book knowledge. Conduct us to your Queen. It may be that we can help her."

In deep thought the old man bowed his head.

To himself he muttered, "No man of magic would make use of a little girl, a simple slate, and a foolish owl. Sore is our strait. Perchance they could assist. I shall risk it. At least, they may serve for a moment to turn the Queen's mind from her misery." Then aloud, "Make no noise; speak no word; but follow me."

With the old warder in the lead, the little party trudged down the passage-way. The air was damp. Moisture dripped from the walls and ceiling. Everything the eye could see was dark, save here and there a sickly light, like a street-lamp on a foggy night.

At length the road opened into a large room, also black and gloomy. In the center of this room, on a curiously carved throne, sat a tiny woman, weeping as though her heart would break. Around her was a crowd of little people, weeping also, and everything on them and about them was black as ink. Here, without a word, the warder vanished.

All were so busy sobbing, and wiping their eyes and noses, that the arrivals were not noticed until Sir Oliver emitted his usual "to who!"

At the sound the lady on the throne arose, brushed the tears from her eyes, and advanced quickly.

"So here are Dollie, Miss Martha, and Sir Oliver Owl," she said, in a mournful tone. "Some time ago my soothsayer foretold your visit, and I made great preparation to entertain you."

"Looks like it," sniffed Miss Martha.

"Hush," whispered Dollie. "You mustn't be imp'lite;" and then she asked, "Won't you please tell me what's the matter and where I am? I b'lieve I'm getting all mixed up."

"You are in the City of Mirth, of which I am Queen," answered the lady.

"Don't strike me as very mirthy. Reminds me more of a graveyard at midnight," interrupted Miss Martha, with another sniff. "And it's so damp no one can tell whether you really are crying, or simply have colds in your heads. I'd rather be entertained at the bottom of a cistern with the top on."

"None of you could have found fault with your reception had you come a few days earlier," continued the Queen. "What you behold is due to a wicked spell cast by my former High Magician, known far and wide as the Magical Man of Mirth. Listen while I relate the sad story of our trouble."

CHAPTER III
A MAGIC BROTH

CHAPTER III

"You must know," commenced the Queen, with difficulty controlling her grief, "that until last night the City of Mirth was all that the name implies. As you yourselves have seen from the earth, the entire cloud was one mass of white, as of purest marble, except at sunrise or sunset, when the walls were painted with pink and gold. The air was dry and balmy, and the breezes, blowing through the passageways, ever made the sweetest music. Sorrow was unknown; there was nothing but song and laughter, dancing and feasting.

"Yesterday the Queen of the City of Joy, on a neighboring cloud, made me a call. Sincere was her praise of my fine home and all that it contains; but when she saw my High Magician, of whom I had been so proud, great was her scorn.

" 'That a *High* Magician,' she cried. 'Why,

41

he doesn't come up to my chin. Mine is at least five feet tall. I wouldn't use yours for anything but a court fool.'

"When she had gone, my wrath burst forth. Calling the man to me, I discharged him and told him to leave and not to return until he was at least six feet in height. He went; but, alas, I had forgotten that I was dealing with a mighty magician. Before going, he called down upon us this fearful curse of gloom and sorrow. That the city and its people are as you see them is due to the wiles of the Magical Man of Mirth."

"I think he's just as mean as he can be," exclaimed Dollie. "But can't we do something for you? Must you be this way always?"

"So I fear," replied the Queen, sadly. "Peace and happiness can come to us only through his death, which could be accomplished by a magic stronger than his own; but who can prepare that, pray?"

"I can," calmly stated Sir Owl.

"Well, you can if you want to," snapped Miss Slate, "but count me out. I'm not going to fool with any magic at my time of life. It isn't respectable."

"I can," repeated Sir Owl, without noticing Miss Slate at all. "I am the wisest being in the whole universe. What I may not know now, I can find out by search and inquiry. Let me suggest that you summon your soothsayer. I would question her. If she can foretell the future, may she not also possess other strange powers?"

"Of course," declared the Queen. "How stupid I am!" She clapped her hands three times; and there approached an ugly old crone, with wrinkled face, toothless gums and straggling wisps of hair. A black wrapper, frayed and stained, flopped and flounced around her limbs, as she stumbled along; and through rents and holes in this sable garment her scrawny throat and arms could be seen. Her lips moved with senseless mutterings, and her watery eyes seemed to be looking far away as though she beheld things hidden from the eyes of others. This was the soothsayer.

"Inform me, good woman," commanded Sir

Owl, "how we can make the magic with which to destroy the wicked man who has brought such grief to your fair city, and how it should be applied to him."

"Why should I answer you?" mumbled the hag. "And yet why not? Even if I tell, you will not know, and I do not fancy the slate nor the little girl will be much help. But it might amuse me to watch your vain efforts. Hearken, now, for I shall speak only once."

Raising herself to her full height, the old witch stretched out one long and scrawny arm so that her forefinger pointed straight at Sir Owl's beak. Then, in hollow tones, she chanted the following verse:

"Take a bone from the mouth of a kingly whale,
A porpoise's fin and a rusty nail,
Place them in a shell with never a crack
And fill it with water that's inky black.
Now stew over water that's scalding hot
By using the shell in place of a pot.
Pour the broth down the throat of this man who is magical,
And he'll meet with a fate that is sudden and tragical."

"Plain enough," agreed the owl. "Thank you for your kindness. You see, my dear Queen, how easy it is to solve a mystery when a wise man, such as you see I am, takes the lead."

"Stuff and nonsense," scolded Miss Martha. "You're as far off as ever, and that witch knows it. Where will you get a bone from the head of a whale? At a department store? Is a porpoise going to come up and ask you to pull off one of his fins? And if you do find these two, and the shell and the nail and the black water and the hot water, where is the magician and how are you to pour the stuff down his throat?"

"Wait a moment, Miss Martha," cried Dollie. "The woman hadn't quit speaking. Now she'll tell us the rest, I'm sure."

"Don't be too sure," croaked she. "The owl asked how to make the magic and how to apply it. I have advised him. To add anything more I must have a peck of white diamonds."

The Queen did not have a single gem that had not been turned black. Of these, she offered a bushel, but the soothsayer refused them with a sneer.

At this Dollie renewed her pleading. "Just one word," she begged; "just one or two little teeny, weeny words."

"Well," growled the soothsayer, "you ought to know that whales and porpoises live in the ocean, and where part of the articles are the rest are also. Don't your books tell you that when a magician conceals himself, he changes into some strange animal? The Magical Man of Mirth may as well be a fish in the sea as anything else. Now I am done," and her jaws snapped together like a steel-trap.

"She means we must search the ocean," shouted Dollie, clapping her hands. "I've always wanted to wade on the beach."

"One thing is certain," announced Miss Martha, "you can't drag me into any wet water. It would swell my frame all out of shape and wash off my eyes and everything else."

"Don't you worry," cried Dollie. "I'll take care of you all right. Just think what a lark we'll have. Now let's see what we must get. I'll count on my fingers: whalebone, porpoise's fin, rusty nail, that's three; put 'em in a shell that doesn't leak, that's four; fill it with black water, that's five; stew over hot water, that's six; pour down the throat of the Magical Man

of Mirth; that's seven,—and seven's a lucky
number. Then we come back here and find
everything dry and shiny, and everybody tickled
and happy. Why, I wouldn't miss it for anything."

"Patience, my companions," counseled the
owl. "We are not entering upon a pleasure trip,
and we must be willing to endure some hard-
ships. Our mission is to proceed under my wise
guidance, wherever it may be necessary, in order
to restore to happiness this Queen and her whole
city. It is clear to me that first we must seek
the ocean. Let us do so, and then plan further."

"But are you sure we can find the ocean?"
asked Dollie, jumping up and down in her
eagerness. "We might bump into the mountains
or land in a desert; and I'm in such a big
hurry!"

"The way is easy," remarked the Queen.
"While we have been talking, the breeze has
wafted us along until now the sea is almost
below us. If you descend at once you will drop
directly on the shore. Make haste, for something whispers to me that you will succeed.

Then return, and you may have as your reward anything within my power to grant."

"We don't want any pay," insisted Dollie. "We just want to show that Magical Man of Mirth that he isn't as smart as he thinks he is. And you're so sweet and dear; I'd like to see you all smiling and laughing," she added wistfully.

But there was no time for more delay. So the Queen at once accompanied her guests to the end of the corridor. There, after brief adieus, Sir Owl, with Dollie and Miss Martha on his back, again set sail. As long as the cloud remained in sight Dollie stood up, while she waved her hand to the Queen, and shouted words of good cheer. When she could be seen nor heard no more Dollie dropped down on her feathery couch and peered over the edge. Before long she could see, far below and a little to one side, a mass of gray and white, which she knew must be the ocean. Soon she could hear the murmur of the waves, and Miss Martha, with evident relish, began to sniff the salty breeze. A short time thereafter all alighted on a stretch of sand against

which the wavelets leaped in foam-crowned ripples.

For a few moments all stood in silence, admir-
ing the beauty of the scene and wondering what
to do next. Then Sir Owl, signaling to Dollie
to follow him, waddled towards a pile of huge
rocks which extended into the ocean, and against
which now and then a stray billow dashed with
deafening roar.

Straight out over these boulders he clambered,
with Dollie close behind. There was a little
shriek from her, as her feet almost slipped on
the smooth stones; a wail from Miss Martha,
who knew she would be shattered by such a fall;
and a snort of disgust from Sir Owl, when a
breaker of unusual size sent a shower of spray
over his head and shoulders; but, finally, all
reached the extreme point in safety. Fortu-
nately, the last rock was so lofty that its upper
surface was perfectly dry. Here they were about
to seat themselves when they noticed a blue-
green object of great size crawling and sprawl-
ing at their feet.

"Halt," shouted the animal, in a military

manner. "Who are you, and what are you doing?"

"I am Sir Oliver Owl," announced the bird grandly. "I am the wisest being in all the world. My companions, Dollie Lane and Miss Martha Slate, know much that is in books. We come to search——"

"Hold on," interrupted Miss Martha. "Before you tell this thing more about us, suppose he lets us know who he is and by what right he questions us. I declare, I didn't want to enter the ocean at all, but if he says I can't, I shall, just to spite him."

This remark of Miss Martha's made the animal very angry. Slowly he raised himself till he sat upright on the end of his tail. Then he reached over and tapped the slate with a vicious claw.

"Who am I?" he repeated. "I am Lieutenant Lobster. That's who I am."

"I don't believe it," cried Dollie. "You're blue-green. Lobsters are red."

"Yes," shouted the Lieutenant, "lobsters are red —when they have been boiled! What do you know about *boiled* lobsters?"

"I AM LIEUTENANT LOBSTER THE SENTINEL OF THE REALMS OF THE OCEAN"

For a few moments no one spoke. Then the Lieutenant managed to stifle his wrath and went on: "But we'll come to that later. I am sentinel at the portal of the Realms of the Ocean. Explain to me why you are here."

"Without in any way admitting your authority to question me, the wisest being in the world," replied Sir Owl, with becoming dignity, "I may say that we plan to search the sea for a bone from the mouth of a whale, a porpoise's fin, a rusty nail, a shell without a crack, some inky black water, and some boiling hot water, so that we may make a mystic broth. Then must we find the Magical Man of Mirth, that we may pour this down his throat and destroy him. Thus shall we restore to happiness the City of Mirth, now indeed a city of sorrow."

"No one enters here who does not first pass an examination and correctly answer my queries," insisted Lieutenant Lobster. "Woe to them who refuse. One of you may act for all. Who is your spokesman? Perhaps it should be the eldest. Miss Slate, you will please announce your age."

"What an impertinent creature!" she retorted, sharply. "But if you must know, it's probably a million years or more. Geologists differ."

"A million years! You're certainly crazy or in your dotage. How old are you, Sir Bird?"

"Four feet and seven inches exactly," replied he, stretching himself to his full height.

"You're deaf or foolish!" roared Lieutenant Lobster. "Now what says the child?"

"Please, sir, I'm ten, going on 'leven."

"And you've more sense than the other two put together. I select you for the examination. Tell me first, did you **ever** catch a fish with a hook and line?"

"Yes, sir; but I make brother Bob put the wiggly worms on my hook," answered she stoutly. She did not intend to be frightened by a mere lobster.

"And leave it to flop around and drown in the air?"

"Not 'zactly. We tie a stick to a string and run the string through the fish's gills and mouth. Then we put him back in the water so he won't spoil before we go home."

"Did you or your brother ever dine on fish?"

"Y-e-s, s-i-r." Dollie was becoming a little less confident.

"Now, think carefully. Did you ever eat a boiled lobster?" The creature leaned forward and fairly screamed these words into the child's ears. What to say she did not know. She would not lie, and if she told the truth she feared the result. Then a bright thought came to her.

"Oh, fudge!" she exclaimed. "This is all silliness. Tell me, Mr. Lieutenant Lobster, did you ever make a meal on live shellfish, or crabs, or small fishes? We like meat, and you know it; you like meat, and we know it, without all this nonsense. Why, I'll bet you've swallowed tiny lobsters. Anyway, we're not cannibals."

At these charges the sentinel turned two or three shades paler. Twice he opened his mouth to speak, and twice no sound came forth. Finally, scratching the top of his head with one claw, he remarked, "Well, you certainly are a bright and good-looking youngster. Yes, I shall pass you on this part of the examination. However, there remains the famous riddle, which you must guess aright or you cannot advance. This is where many have failed."

"Now listen closely," he continued; and, in a sing-song voice he rapidly recited the following lines, keeping time meanwhile with his claws:

"I saw a see-saw by the sea;
A saw, sir, and a saucer.
If the sea saw the see-saw,
And the see-saw saw the sea,
Did the saucer see the saw, sir?"

"How easy!" cried Dollie, gleefully. "Yes, of course. If the sea could see the see-saw, and the see-saw could see the sea, the saucer saw the saw, Sir Lobster, unless he was blind. Now, can't we go along, please? We're in a hurry."

"Gently, gently, my little lady and companions," urged the lobster, whose manner suddenly had changed to one of great politeness. "True, you have passed, and now may explore the Realms of the Ocean, but first you must let me prepare you, else you would meet with harm. Remain where you are and await my return." With this warning, he slid down an opening between two of the boulders.

When he came back he bore between his claws

a half-dozen brushes of different sizes and a tin
can from which the cover had been removed. It
was filled with a golden liquid that resembled
paint, and on the outside was pasted a label
upon which Dollie slowly spelled the following
sentences:

"Lieutenant Lobster's Lo-co-mo-tion Lin-a-ment.
A Sure Aid To Easy Progress.
Upward, Downward, Forward, Backward, Sideways,
Also Prevents Dampness, Chilliness, Wetness,
Or Any Ill Effect From Im-mer-sion in Water.
One Trial Will Convince.
Use No Other."

"This is a powerful fluid," explained Lieutenant Lobster. "When you three go below it will
assist you in breathing and seeing, will protect
your clothing, feathers and bodies from the
water, and will enable you to withstand the
great weight of the ocean above you. If you
become tired of walking on the bottom, it will
help you to glide around, and to rise or to sink,
or to move forward or backward, like fishes.
Dollie, take the brushes and cover Sir Owl thoroughly, also Miss Martha. The stuff will prevent the dampness from destroying her beautiful
features. After being applied, it is absolutely

colorless, so it will not bother you any. Lively, now; and then Sir Owl must do the same for you."

In a few moments all had received, from top to toe, a complete coating of the linament. Then they turned to ask if they now might go on their way.

"One last word," added the Lieutenant. "When you get inside, you will sink to the bottom. Don't become excited, but stand still until you can see, and until you feel somewhat at home; and you better call for Number Thirteen. Yes, be sure to do so. Now good-bye; a fine time to you." And, with a splash, he dived from view.

"You'll go, won't you, Miss Martha?" coaxed Dollie. "It won't hurt you a bit."

"Really, I don't approve at all," answered that cautious lady. "You mark my words, that magic man will get us into a fix yet. But if you're set on it, I give in. Your mother never would forgive me were I not along to take care of you; and I don't trust that owl any more— not for one single minute."

"There sha'nt anything hurt you, darling," said Dollie, hugging Miss Martha in her arms. "Now, let's jump when I count."

Side by side, bird and girl perched on the edge of the rock, while slowly she recited:

> " 'Rickety, jickety, jock,
> Plickety, hickety, hock;
> One, two, three,
> Off—go—we!' "

With the last word, the three plunged beneath the waves.

CHAPTER IV
NUMBER THIRTEEN

CHAPTER IV

Before Dollie leaped she squinted her eyes, and when she struck the water she squealed, "Ouch!" Not that the squint nor the "ouch" did her any good, but that is the way all little girls do when they spring from a high place. Sir Oliver, on the contrary, opened his eyes wider than ever, as became his dignity, and just before he reached the surface he shouted his loudest "to who!" to show his contempt for a salt puddle. Then the sea, in a spirit of sport, tossed a handful of spray down the wrong side of his throat, so that he sputtered and choked all the way until his claws finally rested on the ground. Dollie, still closely hugging Miss Martha, landed safely beside him.

In the dim light at the bottom of the ocean Sir Owl could see perfectly; but Dollie for a few moments was afraid to move, as you are when you suddenly step out into the dark from

61

a lighted room. However, little by little her sight returned, and soon she could distinguish the objects around her quite clearly. The smooth sand beneath her feet shone white and clean. Here and there lay a huge rock or a water-soaked log, and in the distance were moving objects which probably were fishes. You may be sure she was delighted that such a good start had been made in the search for the wicked magician.

Another thing pleased her greatly. While she knew that they were entirely covered, there was no feeling of wetness, nor even of dampness. The mystic liquid kept her perfectly dry; and she found that she could breathe, and move her hands and body as easily as if in the air. Sir Owl's feathers, too, appeared to be light and airy as ever, and Miss Martha's features were still plainly marked and beautiful.

As soon as she had her bearings, her first thought was for her beloved slate.

"How you feeling, Miss Martha?" she asked anxiously. "You look perfectly lovely. There's lots and lots for us to do. Don't you think we better commence right straight off?"

"Yes, indeed," answered Miss Martha, "and have it done with. I didn't want to undertake the job, but we can't turn back now. And before we're through I shall show that owl that I know more than he does; see if I don't. It takes more than big eyes to make a wise bird."

"But wasn't there something Lieutenant Lobster asked us to do right away? Strikes me so, but I can't remember."

"He told us to call Number Thirteen, but whatever he meant's more than I know."

"Of course," cried Dollie; "how dull in me!" Then, in her childish treble, she shouted as loud as she could, "Number Thirteen; NUMBER T-H-I-R-T-E-E-N!"

Immediately a shrill voice from a point about opposite her waist, answered: "That's my name; what can I do for you, please?"

Looking down, she was astonished to behold a tiny fish, not over eight inches long. His whole body trembled with intense excitement; his fins and tail vibrated so rapidly as almost to be invisible; and yet he kept his position right in front of her. Around his eyes were narrow rings of yellow, as if he wore gold-rimmed spectacles. His body was marked with bands of gold and deepest blue, and his fins also were of golden hue.

"Oh, aren't you a beauty!" cried Dollie. "Wish I had you home in a jar of water."

"I'd like to please you," replied the fish, "but I'm glad you haven't, 'cause it'd soon kill me. Say, why did you yell so for me?"

"Lieutenant Lobster said for us to call 'Number Thirteen.' We didn't know that was your name, though."

"Good for him! I'm a pilot fish out of a position. Asked him to boost for me. Couldn't you help a fellow out? I'm a first-rate guide."

'What do you charge?" asked the practical Miss Martha

'Don't charge at all. What I'm after's to find some one who wants to go somewhere. I'll take him, safe and sound." The pilot fish was such a bundle of nerves that his sentences were short and jerky.

"That's cheap enough," Sir Owl asserted. "We'll hire you. I am the wisest being in all the world, and I can find my way anywhere alone; yet a good guide would save me trouble and enable me to fix my mind on weightier matters than the mere path we are to follow."

"Wait a moment," urged Dollie. "We ought to know more about a servant before we take him. Mamma always does."

"Very well," agreed Sir Oliver "I shall ask the questions. You remember how I found out from the soothsayer all about the way to slay the magician." Then to the fish: "How much experience have you had? Where did you work last?"

"Eight years old. Worked seven years straight for the Shark family. That ought to be plenty."

"Why did you quit?"

"Mrs. Shark tried to eat me up. Isn't that 'nough?"

"But if you're a good guide, why did she try to eat you?" persisted Sir Owl.

"Don't like to run down folks who've employed me, but, if you'll all cross your hearts and promise not to tell, I'll give you the whole story."

After everyone had been pledged to secrecy, he commenced: "Last job was for a Mrs. Shark. Got along well for a while. Then we had a fuss. What do you think I found scattered around me one morning? Fifteen little sharklets! And what do you guess she ordered me to do? Nurse 'em and watch over 'em; me, a guide!"

The little fish was so wrought up that it really seemed as though he would fall to pieces, but finally he calmed himself and proceeded: "Worst of it was, when time came for the babies to take a nap, she said I must swim straight down her throat, so they'd follow me. Tried it just once. Dark as a pocket there; no good air; hot and stuffy. Sharklets plumped after me and jammed into me and one another. Rammed me down like a wad in a gun-barrel. When I came out I told Mrs. Shark I'd quit; and I did. Now, don't you want me to guide you?"

"To be sure we do," all exclaimed; and Dollie added: "But we can't call you Number Thirteen. That's too long; and Pilot isn't pretty. Believe we'll dub you Lottie. It's a girl's name, but you won't mind, will you?"

"Not a bit; it's all the same to me if I have a good job. Say, I can't stay still much longer. Let's start; and what do you want first?"

"We seek several things," answered Sir Oliver; "a bone from the head of a whale, a porpoise's fin, a rusty nail, black water, and a shell to hold all of these; then hot water over which to boil them; and finally the Magical Man of Mirth, that we may pour the broth down his throat and kill him."

"W-h-e-w," whistled Lottie. "That's a large order. Must take 'em one at a time. Saw some porpoises around here a few days ago. Let's look for 'em."

"I say," replied Dollie, thoughtfully, "that we ought to practice a wee bit before we go very far. Lottie, you scoot 'round us if you want to, or run away for a spell. We aren't the least mite afraid."

Sir Owl insisted that a bird of his wisdom did not need any practice. By flapping his wings he could swim as far and as fast as he could fly. Miss Martha, to her great joy, found that when she turned edgeways Lieutenant Lobster's Linament enabled her to cut through the water like a knife. However, Dollie, who is plump and chubby, had more to learn.

After a few false steps she could tread the hard, firm sand without any trouble. It was no more difficult than walking on land. But when she tried to rise above the bottom and to swim, she met with difficulty, and tossed around without making any headway.

In the midst of her efforts, Lottie, quieted by his spin, returned. "What are you trying to do, anyway?" he asked. "Swim like a fish? Let me show you. Don't kick and flop so. When you want to go up, fill your lungs full of air and take long, deep breaths; when you want to come down, force out the air and take little breaths. Elbows close to your sides; use your hands like fins; wave them from front to back, and you start forward; from back to front, backward; and steer with your feet. Now once more."

With her chest puffed out as suggested, Dollie swiftly soared far towards the surface. By paddling with her hands, she went ahead faster than before, and she even could go backward a little. Sir Owl and Miss Martha followed.

"That's good," cried Lottie, who kept hovering near. "You need experience, but soon you'll be nimble as any fish in the pond. Be careful about keeping your balance. If you aren't, you'll find your heels above your head first thing you know."

This last remark tickled Dollie, and caused her to lose control over herself. As a result, she forgot to keep her lungs inflated regularly, and in a moment she dropped suddenly to the bottom, where she lit with a thud, though not hard enough to cause a bruise.

"Better look out," Lottie advised. "Long as you have that magic stuff, you can't fall and hurt yourself; but you ought to prepare to enter the best submarine society. How's that for elegant language?"

"She can fall hard enough to hurt me," snarled a muffled voice which apparently came from beneath the ground. "And will she please take her heel off the small of my back?"

Dollie immediately spread both of her feet as far apart as possible and gazed between them.

A pointed head, with protruding, beady eyes, was working up through the sand near one of her shoes. Somehow the head had a familiar look, but she was not sure until a big claw also stuck up and waved around as if it wanted to pinch something.

"It's Lieutenant Lobster," whispered Dollie to Miss Martha, "but don't you talk to him till he cools off. 'Member how I keep quiet when Uncle Tom's riled?"

There was absolute silence while the object, little by little, crawled from its nest. When entirely emerged, it was easy to see that Dollie was right; but all waited for the Lieutenant to speak.

After shaking himself, as a dog does when he has come out from the water, he turned to face those who, as he thought, had been teasing him; and when he spoke, his frame quivered with rage.

"What do you mean, you young rascal?" he screamed at Dollie. "You find my resting-place in the dirt here; then you go up a mile or two and try to drop onto me like a pile-driver. I'd as lief be caught in a trap and boiled in a pot as be squashed to death. And when you miss me, you sit down and kick me in the back. Consider yourself under arrest."

"Very well, sir," replied Dollie.

At the sound of the girl's voice the lobster gave a jump, and, as if to clear his vision, began to rub his eyes with his claws.

"Bless my shell," he exclaimed, "if here aren't Dollie, Miss Martha, Sir Oliver Owl, and Number Thirteen also! Well, well! I can't get mad at Dollie. Reckon she was trying to swim, and had a tumble."

"That's a fact," said she. "But why did you bury yourself in that hole?"

"Taking a sand bath for my gout. Nothing does me so much good. My, I feel fifty years younger already! It's well I do, for I've tough work on hand."

"What is it?" asked Dollie. "Can't we help you?

"Some two miles from here, fast on the reefs, lies an old wreck, on which dwell a merman, a merwoman, and the cutest little mermaid you ever saw. All their lives these three have laughed and sung, as jolly as a pack of school-children at recess. But of late they have taken to sobbing, groaning and shrieking, till they're a public nuisance. It is my duty to make them behave. Friends of mine complain, too, because from what was the captain's cabin floats, night and day, a hideous yowling. This also I am about to look into; and, if you care to go along, I should be right glad to have your company."

"We could pick up a rusty nail somewhere around that wreck," suggested Miss Martha; "and on the way we might meet some porpoises."

"That is correct," Sir Owl assented. "What you have learned from books really does help you at times. And I should like to question the merman. It is the part of true wisdom never to scorn aid from any source, however humble. Let us proceed."

The order of their going was arranged easily. Lottie, who knew the way to the wreck, took the lead. Sir Owl, because of his wisdom, claimed second place. Miss Martha and Dollie followed, side by side. Lieutenant Lobster, on account of his age, was not fond of exertion, so he was allowed to cling by one claw to Sir Owl's tail, or to Dollie's sash.

"Forward, march," commanded the Lieutenant. "To-who!" tooted the owl; and thus the little army began its journey.

CHAPTER V

THE RESCUE OF ANN

CHAPTER V

THE RESCUE OF ANN

"I do hope that merman doesn't smoke a hookah," said Miss Martha to Dollie, as they swam along together. "He may be a Turk, for all I know, and you've read how Turks use those disagreeable water-pipes. Smoke gets into one's clothes and hair, and truly I couldn't stand it."

"Don't worry about that," answered the child. "There isn't anything here to strike a match on, and it isn't the right kind of a place, either. In a book at home there's a picture of a caterpillar sitting on a toadstool and smoking a hookah. Toadstools grow where it's damp, but not with water all over 'em. 'Tisn't a good plan to borrow trouble, anyway," she concluded, wisely.

But conversation soon ceased, because all became interested in looking about them. They saw that the sand was becoming blacker and that the rocks and boulders were more plentiful.

After they had gone about a mile, sharp reefs often reached up almost to Dollie's feet, and between these reefs were valleys so deep that the bottom could not be descried.

"Better not look down," Miss Martha cautioned Dollie. "You might get mixed up or dizzy and have another tumble. Remember how easily you can walk across a bridge on the ties if you don't glance at the current? This is just the same."

"All right, dear," answered Dollie; "but I'm feeling dandy."

Soon could be heard the pounding of the surf on a rocky shore, and above it all the shrieks and cries of the merman family. A little farther along, the yowling also could be distinguished. Lottie now darted behind Dollie, and immediately she felt three sharp pulls on her sash. This was the Lieutenant's signal for stopping. Below them, on the summit of a cliff, was a smooth space to which they rapidly lowered themselves.

"I only tried to tell you we're 'most there," said Lottie; "what did you quit for?"

"That yowling bothers me," admitted the Lieutenant. "I can deal with the merman and his folks, because they can be seen and touched and arrested; but every fish who has examined the old ship says there's nothing to cause that other sound. How can I punish a mere noise? Will someone please tell me?"

"Listen a moment," cried Dollie. After an instant's stillness she shouted: "It's a cat, that's what it is. An old cat shut up somewhere on the boat. Afraid of a cat; oh, my!" And she rolled on the rock, from laughter.

"Why, Dollie Lane," disputed Miss Martha, "that boat's been sunk for years and years. A cat would be drowned, even if it does have nine lives."

"Oh, pshaw!" replied Dollie; "you can't fool me. That's a cat's yell sure enough, and the cat itself must be there, too. Sounds just like my Ebenezer."

"Cats are abominable creatures. They destroy nests and eat little birds. This one shall feel my vengeance. If you fear to follow, I shall go on alone," shrieked Sir Owl, ruffling his feathers angrily.

No danger of that; already Lottie had led off, and the Lieutenant, zealous as the rest, grabbed Dollie's sash, as she and Miss Martha followed.

Dollie could now swim much more rapidly and with less effort than at the commencement of the journey. In their eagerness, all fairly dashed along, so that her sash, with Lieutenant Lobster attached, trailed out far behind.

The reefs slowly gave way to the yellow and white sand again; and Lottie, the others close behind him, sank till near the bottom. In a few moments they came to an immense mass of jagged rocks which pierced the surface. Against this barrier the waves beat with angry growls, and even below, the water seemed to be troubled as by the presence of an enemy.

Here another halt was made. "This is Dead Man's Point," explained Lottie. "Wreck's on the other side. All we have to do is to swim 'round. Any orders, Lieutenant?"

"Forward is the word," cried that doughty warrior. "Take us to the ship. You three will wait below, while with Sir Owl I mount the deck and approach the merman and his family.

A few words with them will enable us to make our plans. When needed, you shall be summoned. Forward, march!"

After passing the Point, the expedition found itself almost against the vessel. Here, brave Lieutenant Lobster moved himself from Dollie's sash to Sir Owl's tail, and, without one backward look, both shot upward and disappeared upon the deck.

Their absence gave the others, resting on the sand, a chance to view the wreck at their leisure. Pitiful, indeed, was the sight. Head on, the good ship had hit the reef above with force enough to stave in her hull half-way to the stern. Then, slipping back, she must have sunk immediately.

Curious barnacles and sea-weed covered her sides. Her masts had fallen, and some of the broken fragments, buried in the dirt, still were partly visible. Not a trace of the sails could be seen. The name on her bow had gone when she struck, and if one had been on her stern also, it had been effaced by the action of the elements.

Poor old ship! Time was when on sunny days and moonlight nights, with all canvas set, light as a bird she had sped before the welcome breeze. Now, shattered and dismantled, gradually she was falling to pieces, unnoticed and unmourned.

Thoughts like these passed through Dollie's mind, and queer little thrills of sympathy played around her heart; but the time for dreaming was short. At the edge of the deck appeared the form of Lieutenant Lobster, and with clarion clearness rang forth his order, "Reserves, advance!"

Nor was the command unwelcome. Quick as quick could be, Dollie and Miss Martha lightly soared and joined their officer. Then, for the first time, they noticed the noise, except from the cabin, had ceased.

"It's all strategy," chuckled the Lieutenant; "great thing for an army. Told the merman and his wife that I was bringing a girl from the earth to call on them, and that they mustn't disgrace themselves by such a racket. They stopped instantly, and are trying to act pleasant, though it seems to be hard work. I'll introduce you, and then we'll go below and look into the yowling first."

After all had been made acquainted, Miss Martha and Dollie found it difficult to refrain from staring rudely at the merman and woman, who were reclining on the deck near the stern. The body of each above the middle was without clothing; from the waist down, it was covered by a flowing garment of woven sea-weed, below the bottom of which protruded a tail like Lottie's, only larger. This showed that the creatures were half human and half fish.

A mass of curly, yellow locks crowned the man's head and fell around his shoulders. A bushy, tawny beard rested on his breast. The woman, too, had long golden hair, which she kept smoothing continually with a shell comb; and around her neck hung a magnificent coral necklace, with some queer object like a locket swinging from its center.

"Whatever is that funny thing dangling over her bosom?" inquired Miss Martha, whose sharp eyes missed nothing. "It looks like sole leather.

Don't you know, Lottie? A good guide ought to tell about everything without waiting to be asked."

Lottie's reply, however, was cut off by the Lieutenant's sharp command: "To the cabin; forward, march!"

Immediately upon entering the room formerly occupied by the captain, it was certain that the sound had its origin there. From the walls, the floor and the ceiling—all about them it floated. But what made it? There was no place for concealment. The desk, the chairs and the locker had been tipped over and broken into pieces by the force of the crash. All the pictures except one, the likeness of an officer in full uniform, had fallen from their places. Where could be hidden anything capable of causing such an outcry?

The whole army made a most careful search, but to no purpose. They peeped and they peered, they scratched and they clawed, they ordered and they tooted, but all to no avail. After they had poked into every nook and corner, the solution seemed as far away as ever.

Meanwhile the unearthly wailing kept on, right in their ears. Do you wonder that Dollie, and even Miss Martha, began to feel somewhat scared?

Then Lottie had a scheme of his own. Beginning in exactly the center of the floor, round and round he swam in constantly increasing squares. When he reached the walls, he climbed them in the same way, little by little, an inch or two higher each time. Nothing happened until he passed the portrait. There he paused, listened, went on, came back, listened again, and then rushed frantically to the Lieutenant.

"The sound comes from inside that picture!" he shouted; "have Dollie bring it down."

Dollie did not delay. In a jiffy she had the picture on the floor, where it immediately was surrounded by the eager group.

When this had taken place, the wailing ceased; but imagine the surprise when a cross voice, apparently from inside the frame, complained: "Well, if some one has found me, why doesn't some one let me out?"

"Who are you, anyway, and how shall we do

it?" asked Dollie, trembling with excitement.

"Never mind who I am. Take a stone or something and straighten the ends of the nails where they are clinched; then take off the back."

Dollie did as directed; and gave a scream of amazement. In plain view before her, pierced by the brads, lay the outline of a cat, and this outline was filled by a misty substance that looked like smoke. This it was that had spoken, because with the next words its jaws moved.

"I'm stuck to the paper and glass," it said. "Pry me off, as your mother lifts a pie from the tin. Be careful not to tear me."

Again Dollie did as bidden. Lieutenant Lobster and Sir Owl, with their claws, helped by holding up the parts that she had worked loose. When they had finished, the shadow of a cat stood in front of them. It yawned, gave its tail a switch, and scratched an ear with one foot, just as any tabby does when aroused.

"Now that we've got you off and out," said Miss Martha, "I think you'd better tell us all about yourself and what you were doing in that funny place. You're certainly the oddest thing

I've seen in all my life. How did you get here?"

"And I command you to," added the Lieutenant, "for I have been sent here to put a stop to your terrible noise."

"I'm the ghost of a cat, if you're so curious," said the object, "and if you want me to spin my yarn, here it is. Years ago, when alive, the sailors on this ship took me with them as mascot; but the captain never liked me. One night he threw me overboard and I was drowned. To get even, I haunted him. You ought to have seen him jump when I tipped his ink-pot over, or upset his bottle of rum.

"But he came out ahead without knowing it. The front and the back of this picture had fallen apart a few inches, and I liked to sleep in the space between them. One day, while I was napping, the captain made the cabin-boy mend the frame, and the nails pierced my body. That fixed me. A ghost can go from place to place without minding wood or glass, but a piece of steel through a ghost pins him tight, like a butterfly on a card. That's a fact, and I couldn't get out."

The ghost again yawned and scratched its head; then it continued: "That very night the ship sank on these rocks. All hands, except the captain, saved themselves. He was drowned, which tickled me 'most to death."

"Can ghosts die?" asked Lottie, with a puzzled look.

"Don't interrupt me," was the answer. "I had to stay in that horrid picture till some one released me. Now I'd like to know who you are, and what you are about."

"I am Lieutenant Lobster," replied that individual, "sent here to quell the disturbance. Let Sir Owl speak for the others."

That he was right glad to do. "I am Sir Oliver Owl, the wisest being in all the world," he began as usual. "With Dollie and Miss Martha Slate, who know what is in books, I seek a rusty nail——"

"Not now," interrupted Dollie. "One of those in the picture frame was all rusty and Miss Martha told me to put it in my pocket."

"Very well," announced the owl. "A fine start has been made. That is what comes from having me at the head of the expedition. Now we still need a porpoise's fin, a bone from a whale's head, a shell without a crack, black water, hot water, and then the Magical Man of Mirth, that we may pour the mixture down his throat and destroy him and his wicked spells. For these things, after having talked with the merman and his wife, we shall search the ocean far and wide."

"Let me go, too," requested the ghost. "I've been cooped up so long, a little excitement will do me good. And I'll find some way to help you, never fear."

"You may come," replied Sir Owl. "I hate cats and the ghosts of cats, but in the interest of science I control my passion. In me you behold the President of the Omnipotent Order of Omniscient Owls. At its last meeting, when there were present seven furlongs and thirty-three rods of birds, I delivered an address on the 'Habits and Haunts of Ghosts I Have Met.' All agreed it was the most whooping speech they ever had heard. Now, I can examine you at my leisure, and obtain facts which will add to my renown. So I give you permission to come."

"But we must have your name, please," Dollie remarked, "unless you want us to call you 'Kittie.'"

"Miss Cat; Miss Ann Gora Cat, if you'd rather have the full name."

"Then we'll christen you Ann, if you don't care. That'll do nicely."

"Makes no difference to me. I'm not at all stuck up."

"You were stuck up behind that picture, all right," snickered Lottie.

"Let joking cease," shouted the Lieutenant. "Duty beckons. We must perform the remainder of our mission. Forward, march!"

CHAPTER VI

THE ATTACK ON THE SEA SERPENT

CHAPTER VI

THE ATTACK ON THE SEA SERPENT

When the deck had been reached again, it was not the Lieutenant nor Sir Owl, but Miss Martha, who took the lead in questioning the merman and his wife.

"Whatever do you mean by hanging that piece of ugly leather below your throat?" asked she. "If you are trying to dress up, a nice shirt waist would be far better; and if you are afraid you will catch cold, try a strip of red flannel or chamois skin. Leather makes good shoes, but you don't seem to have any feet to use 'em on."

"I wear it," replied the merwoman, "for a charm to prevent malaria, as you might put a potato in your pocket, or a brass ring on your finger, to guard against rheumatism. You may have noticed that the climate here is apt to be damp and chilly at certain seasons of the year. This dolphin's fin, which you observe, tends to keep me well."

"A dolphin's fin!" shouted Dollie. "Oh, please give it to me. I want it for a very partic'lar purpose."

"A dolphin's fin!" re-echoed Sir Owl. "I knew it all the time. How easily a wise person may find whatever he seeks."

"We prize it too highly to bestow it lightly upon anyone by whom it may be desired," announced the merman. "There is only one way in which all of you might earn it and at the same time Lieutenant Lobster would remove the cause of our grief so that once more we should laugh and sing."

"Tell us immediately," commanded the Lieutenant. "We should rather deserve it through some mighty deed than to take it from you by force."

"Then give ear unto my words," said the merman. "Happy were the days when our daughter, the beautiful mermaid Minerva, lay at our feet and mingled the music of her voice with ours. Now she is gone. Restore her to us, and the fin is yours. But, alas, I fear that never shall we behold her again!"

"Twaddle," replied the Lieutenant. "Furnish me the facts, and be she alive, I and my brave comrades will return her to you safe and sound."

"Not far from here," the merman explained, "is a coral reef of great size. It is square in shape and hollow in the center. In the vacant space a sea-serpent has his lair. The sole entrance is a tunnel, only large enough to admit his body. Our fair daughter has been stolen by this horrid monster and taken to this retreat. There she will stay, because rescue is out of the question. No one can force his way through the coral, and her master leaves his home no more.

"Faithful servants bring him food. In case of danger, he waits with his horny head just without the hole. Thus the rest of him is protected. His eyes flash fire, his forked tongue lashes the water, and his hot, poisonous breath causes it to foam and boil. To save her is impossible; our child is lost forever."

"Do not think so," answered the Lieutenant. "The task, indeed, is a difficult one, but I doubt not we shall find some way to fool the beast. What say you, my bold soldiers?"

"If we can't get ahead of a naughty old snake I think we'd better go right home," was Dollie's opinion, to which the others gave prompt assent.

"Then let us march at once," decided Lieutenant Lobster. "As has been the case with the wreck, we can arrange our plans better after we have reached the scene of action. Meanwhile, my mournful couple, you will restrain yourselves. If we hear any more shrieks we shall cease the work of relief. Be quiet, and soon your child will be with you again. Now, are all ready?"

"Wait a moment," cried Dollie, as she disappeared down the hatchway that led to the forecastle. When she returned, she proudly bore a dagger not much larger than a thick wire and no longer than a knitting needle. With this she poked and jabbed the water, as if she were attacking someone with a hat-pin. If she could only stick her little rod of steel into one of the monster's eyes, that would be the end of him.

This warlike preparation pleased the Lieutenant, but he was anxious about the location of the robber's den. Lottie said he never had noticed it, and he feared there might be some delay in finding the exact place.

"Haven't you been there?" Dollie asked Ann, who was standing close beside her. But Ann, too, was ignorant. Dollie looked away for an instant, and then chanced to glance down again. Ann was gone.

"Why, where's Ann?" she cried. "She was right by my feet not a second ago."

"She's there now," laughed Miss Martha. "Where are your eyes?"

True enough. The cat ghost stood in her former position, as though she had not moved at all. This puzzled Dollie, but Ann only grinned.

"I have been to the snake's home," she announced, in a matter-of-fact tone.

"But you haven't had time," blurted Sir Owl.

"It doesn't take a ghost any time to go from one place to another. I wished myself at the reef, and I was there. I peered around for an instant; that was when you missed me. Then I wished myself back, and here I am, ready to help Lottie guide you."

"But if you went and returned in such a manner," insisted Sir Owl, "you couldn't have marked the route, and can't remember it. All cats are selfish and treacherous. I do not trust you for one moment."

"You're bright for an owl," answered Ann, haughtily, "but you don't know everything. You might make notes now for your next whooping speech. Dollie is aware of the fact that on earth one can carry a cat in a covered basket miles and miles from home, but she always finds her way back without trouble. As a cat ghost, the same power is mine. I've visited the snake's lair, and I'm able to return to it directly, even if I didn't note the road."

"Let her have a trial," advised the Lieutenant. "Ann, take your place by Lottie's side. Too much time has been wasted. Forward, march!"

The trip was exceedingly pleasant. Once more beneath them lay the white sand, smooth and level as a carpet. An angry surf no longer lashed and roared. Instead, the waves murmured softly as they curled and broke upon the surface.

At times the party approached near enough to

the top to see the twinkling stars and to watch
their soft light glitter on the ripples. So en-
tranced were Dollie and Miss Martha by the ex-
quisite beauty and harmony of their surroundings
that they forgot entirely the warlike mission on
which they were bent, until a few words from
Ann brought them back to the real object of the
expedition.

"We've covered the greater part of the distance," said she. "Straight out from here, towards the middle of the ocean, lies the spot we
seek. How do I know? Because I *know*. Don't
ask me silly questions."

A sharp turn to the right, and the little army
swam out to sea. There was perfect silence.
Doubtless each member was trying to think how
he or she could aid best in the battle that seemed
necessary, for no one believed that the serpent
would give up his prize without a desperate
struggle.

At length there could be seen, far ahead, what
looked like a gigantic pillar of white marble,
which extended from the earth to the surface of
the sea. At a closer view the pillar increased to

the size of a city square; and, instead of marble, it evidently was made of coral. As this seemed to be the point they sought, the Lieutenant ordered a halt. After an instant's pause, the rescuers, walking on the bottom, advanced slowly; but no sign of tunnel or snake could be perceived.

"I knew we should be led astray," grumbled Sir Owl. "Who ever heard of a cat doing anything right?"

"It's the place we're after," Ann assured him. "I remember now that the rascal and his hole are on the side opposite from the shore."

When this important matter had been settled, it was a joy to notice how confidently Lieutenant Lobster, who, being an officer, was to have charge of the attack, laid his plans.

"We must examine this wall before us," said he, "every foot of it, and see if there is not some secret passage through which we can enter and bring out the mermaid without giving alarm."

The search, however, was fruitless. Not a crevice large enough to admit even Lottie's small body could be detected.

"Now, let us divide," continued the zealous officer. "Sir Owl, Lottie, and Ann, take the side to the left; Dollie, Miss Martha, and I will look over the one to the right. Then we will meet beyond the front of the structure. Remember, we must be on our guard. The wretch might dash out and nab one of us."

When re-united, all made the same report. Not a crack nor a hole big enough to be of any account had been discovered.

"Well," counseled the Lieutenant, "let us not be disheartened. There is the more chance to win glory. If you look sharply you can see the mouth of the tunnel midway between the corners and about twenty feet from the ground. The enemy's head is just within. It is my duty to approach and demand the surrender of the mermaid. Dollie and Sir Owl may escort me. The rest of you, await our return."

"I treat with no villain who destroys eggs and little birds," insisted Sir Owl, hotly. "With this cat-ghost Ann, I am on terms of peace in the cause of science; but I shall meet this snake only to scratch his face with my claws and to peck out his eyes with my beak. Here I remain until it is time to fight."

So Dollie and the Lieutenant went forth alone. Tightly grasping her trusty dagger, the child strode up to a short distance from the citadel. Then the Lieutenant, standing on the very tip of his tail, on the very top of her head, called out loudly: "Sir Serpent! Sir Serpent! Come forth and listen to my words!"

Without making any verbal reply, the monster thrust his horny head and scaly shoulders out from the mouth of the cavern. There he awaited the message.

"I am here," announced the lobster, "to command the instant release of the mermaid whom you have imprisoned."

Instead of becoming angry, the serpent grinned from ear to ear; then he laughed till his shoulders shook.

"What if I refuse?" he asked.

"I shall arrest you," shouted the officer; "and if you resist, I shall put you to death."

At this threat the monster continued his violent mirth. Finally, he managed to gasp: "Be

off with you, Lobby, before I get mad. Think
of a girl, a slate, an owl, a pilot-fish, the ghost
of a cat, and a fussy jumping-jack like you trying to kill a full-grown animal like me! If I
wait for you as executioners I shall live forever,
unless I die from laughter. Run home now; I'm
going to sleep;" and he drew within.

To be made fun of in this manner was more
than the Lieutenant could endure. The blood
rushed to his head, and he would have fallen to
the ground had not Dollie caught him; but re-
covering pluckily, he grabbed the end of her
sash and ordered a retreat. All the way she
could hear him muttering, "Fussy jumping-jack,
am I? Run home, shall I? I'll show him who I
am before I'm through with him."

When they reached the others, the Lieutenant
had recovered his composure; but Lottie was
found in a state of great anxiety, because Ann
was missing. Without a word to him, she had
left them, and her unexplained absence made
him fear that harm had befallen her.

"Don't say I didn't warn you," hooted Sir
Owl. "I told you so. Cats can kill little birds.

Otherwise they are nothing but cowards."

"Never mind," said the commander; "though the army has lost one-sixth of its strength, still shall that scornful robber feel my power. Let us keep quiet for a few moments and each try to discover some good scheme."

But it was impossible to think clearly. Immediately there arose an uproar from the serpent's castle. His head and shoulders could be seen sticking out from the tunnel, and this time he was in great wrath. His jaws snapped open and shut; his forked tongue cut the water like a lash; the hot breath from his nostrils mingled in circling wreaths of mist with the poisonous gases that escaped from his mouth. A more hideous picture of anger could not be imagined. What had happened?

In the midst of this sudden commotion, Ann, with a broad smile on her face, made her appearance. "It's all too funny," she gasped. "Don't ask me any questions, but wait till I catch my breath."

"Now I'll tell you all there's time for," she went on in a moment. "I visited the mermaid.

She's alive, well, and worth saving. When satisfied of that, I examined the creature himself. His body ends in a long tail no bigger than a rope. The rest of it, while large as a barrel, seems nothing but skin, with here and there a rib to hold it up, like a half-open umbrella. This covering waves and bends as though the inside were full of gas or hot air. The head, shoulders and front legs are the only solid parts. The rest of him is the same as a balloon."

"But I must hurry," continued Ann. "Miss Martha had put a bright idea into my head. I had the mermaid tie his slim tail securely to a stout piece of coral. Thus he can't move out to attack us. Our plan is to tease him all we can. Get as close as possible, without going within reach of his jaws. The point is to make him angry, *angry*, ANGRY! You'll understand."

"Forward, march! Charge!" rang forth the voice of the commander; and none held back.

Then occurred a battle such as never before was waged on land or sea. Without paying any attention to the noxious vapors, and barely keeping clear of the deadly, cutting tongue, Dollie essayed to jab the enemy in the eyes with her dagger; the Lieutenant, clinging to her shoulder with one claw, made frantic efforts with the other to pinch the swaying tongue; Miss Martha, floating here and there, shrieked shrilly; Lottie dashed hither and thither in bewildering circles; Ann found lodgment near the monster's ear and yowled into it dismally; while Sir Owl tooted and pecked and scratched, but ever at a safe distance.

This concerted action, and the knot in his tail, enraged the serpent beyond all bounds. Each instant he waxed more and more wroth, and the water around him grew more and more polluted. Still there were no signs of weakening among the besiegers; but how much longer they could have held out had not the end come unexpectedly, must be a matter of doubt. Suddenly, with a roar like the bursting of a boiler, the ocean was rent by a fierce explosion; and when the mist had cleared away, in front of them, his head and massive shoulders hanging over the edge of the entrance he had protected so stoutly, lay the serpent, dead.

"I knew it!" cried Ann. "Again am I victorious!" shouted the Lieutenant. "Behold the result of my wisdom!" roared Sir Owl. But Dollie, Miss Martha and Lottie, too tired to talk, dropped to the bottom and threw themselves on the sand. Here they were soon joined by the others, and Ann was asked to throw what light she could on the curious end of the fight.

"It's easy as a-b-c, but the credit all belongs to Miss Martha," said she. "When the snake got mad, something inside of him began to make gas faster than it could escape from his mouth. That caused his body to swell and swell. This increase in size continued until by-and-by some part of the thin skin was pressed against a sharp point of coral. That made a puncture, just as in the tire of an automobile; his body blew open, the water rushed in, and there was the end of Mr. Snake. I told the mermaid to untie the knot soon as she heard a big noise, and I reckon she's done so. See, he has fallen to the ground, and the tunnel is clear."

However, it was not necessary for anyone to enter. Without waiting for assistance, the charming mermaid glided forth; earnestly she thanked her preservers for her rescue and praised them for their skill and boldness, every bit of which Sir Owl took unto himself.

Then, with the joyous mermaid in the lead, the victorious army began its triumphant march back to the wreck, there to claim as a reward the precious fragment of a dolphin's fin.

CHAPTER VII
HOW MR. WHALE WAS OUTWITTED

CHAPTER VII

HOW MR. WHALE WAS OUTWITTED

Happy indeed were the merman and his wife when their daughter, fresh and unharmed, appeared before them on the deck of the old wreck. Their thanks to her rescuers seemed too deep for words; but the merwoman, remembering her promise, was quick to detach the piece of dolphin's fin from her necklace, and to hand it to Dollie, who thrust it into her pocket, with the rusty nail. Now she had two of the things needed for the mystic broth.

Then all proceeded to make merry. The merman brought forth a stringed instrument which looked like a harp and struck up a rollicking tune, while his wife, the merwoman, accompanied him by using her comb as a mouth-organ. The mermaid and Miss Martha sang sweetly; Ann meowed softly, and as sweetly as possible; Lottie circled around, as he always did when pleased or excited; and Dollie danced gaily here and there until finally she was entirely out of breath.

As she sank exhausted to the deck, the others, too, became silent, while Lieutenant Lobster, with a wave of one claw, asked for attention.

"So far I have not been able to take an active part in the celebration," said he. "In my younger years I could both dance and sing, but now my voice is hoarse, and when I attempt to hop about, my feelers, claws, legs and tail are apt to become tangled. But if you will listen, I will recite a poem which may amuse and interest you. First, let me ask a question. What is a toucan?"

"A toucan," answered Dollie, "is a bird that lives in the tropics and has a great big bill and beautiful feathers."

"And how large is a tea-can?"

"Why, they're all kinds of sizes." Dollie wondered if her friend were losing his mind.

"Did you ever see a tea-can large enough for a toucan to live in?"

"Yes, I think I have, lots of 'em," replied Dollie, trying to humor him.

"You marvel at my questions," continued the

Lieutenant. "Since the fierce conflict in which I was recently engaged, my mind, as often happens in such cases, has been going back over boyhood days. In my youth I attended a military academy, and I remember how our professor of logic, who was a poet as well, proved to us one day that all who dwell in the ocean could live in one tea-can. The jingle is running through my head now. Let me repeat it:

> " 'If one toucan finds that he can
> Live in comfort in a tea-can,
> Then you, too, can do what he can;
> If you two can, surely three can;
> And if three can, why, then, four can;
> So if four can, many more can.
> Thus all who live in the sea can
> Dwell in comfort in one tea-can.'

Now, that's logic, so the professor said, but it doesn't sound right to me. What's wrong with it?"

"Don't ask me," replied Dollie. "I never studied logic, and we mustn't talk school, anyway; it's too dry. Here's the only poem I know," and, jumping on a rock as though it were a platform, she recited in a piping voice:

"Simple Simon went a-fishing
    For to catch a whale;
But all the water that he had
    Was in his mother's pail."

This outburst of Dollie's was greeted with shouts of laughter from everyone; that is, from everyone but Sir Owl. During all the celebration he had been sitting off by himself, motionless, with his head drawn down between his wings. Now he suddenly stalked into the center of the group of merry-makers and commenced one of his pompous speeches.

"I have permitted all this nonsense," announced he, "because it seems to give you pleasure. As for myself, such proceedings are beneath my dignity, especially in company with a detestable cat, even though a ghost. But understand me, I have refrained through unwillingness, not through lack of ability. I can do everything better than anyone else. I can dance with more grace, I can sing with more sweetness than the best of you. Let me give you a proof of my superior wisdom. Dollie and the Lieutenant have spoken pieces told to them by others or read in books. Meanwhile, I, standing apart, have made up this poem of my own—every word and idea original.   Mark it well, for it will live forever:

> "Miss Martha Slate, it is sad to relate,
>   Knows nothing not written in books,
> While Miss Dollie Lane, it is equally plain,
>   Isn't nearly as bright as she looks.
> That ghost of a cat, she does'nt know scat,
>   And Lottie is only a guide;
> The Lobster is old, and, though somewhat bold,
>   His folly I cannot abide.
> I, Sir Oliver Owl, am a very wise fowl,
>   A very wise fowl am I.
> Wide open to me are the things of the sea,
>   And the earth, and the realms of the sky.
> The fin and the nail and the bone from a whale
>   Are easy for *me* to obtain;
> Black water and hot, and a shell for a pot,
>   Come quickly to one with *my* brain.
> Let that Magical Man hide wherever he can;
>   His efforts most surely shall fail,
> Since I, the wise owl, the intelligent fowl,
>   Am shrewdly pursuing his trail."

"Whatever does that silly bird mean by such a string of words?" asked the merman, when Sir Oliver had finished. "He did not discover the fin. Miss Martha did that. And my good wife gave it to Dollie, as was proper. But what is all this about a bone, a shell, different kinds of water, and a Magical Man in hiding?"

"We've come down here," replied Dollie, "to find a wicked magician, the Magical Man of Mirth. He worked for the Queen of the City of Mirth, in a most beautiful cloud. Well, she discharged him and then he got mad and cast a spell over the city so that it's all dark and sloppy and everybody cries all the time. An old witch says he's hiding in the ocean and told us how to make a magic broth to spill down his throat and kill him. We've got two of the things already—a rusty nail and a dolphin's fin. Now we need a bone from a whale's head, some black water, a shell to put 'em all in, and some hot water to stew 'em over. You've lived here ever and ever so long. Where do you think we better look next?"

Thoughtfully the merman stroked his long beard, and for some moments he pondered deeply. Then he replied, "There are plenty of whales not far south from here. But how to remove a bone from the head of one of them is a serious question. In the same neighborhood you may come across a lady turtle. Follow her and she will take you to an island where you will find the desired shell. I should look for black water near the caverns in the very uttermost depths of the ocean, and there mayhap is hiding the Magical Man of Mirth. But the hot water may lead you on a long and perilous journey. There is a legend in our family that if one swims south, and ever farther and farther south, he will come to a point where to proceed he must go north. How this can be, I know not, but I tell it to you as it has been told to me. And there, it is said, is a spring which eternally boils and bubbles. Take my advice, little girl, and go home. The task is a dangerous one, and not for such as you."

"Go home now," cried Dollie; "when we've just started! Why all the girls would call me a 'fraid cat.' And we promised the Queen that we'd make her all happy again. You've helped us a whole lot, and I thank you ever so much, but I think we must be finding the shell and all the other things. Don't you, Miss Martha?"

"Indeed I do, but if we never get back, you mustn't blame me. That owl gets crazier and crazier every minute, and we can't rely much on a little fish, a cat-ghost, and a lobster so old that his joints creak." These last remarks she made in a low tone, so that she was not overheard.

At this point the Lieutenant would brook no further delay. "Fall in!" he shouted; "To who!" tooted Sir Owl; and once more the adventurers set forth in the usual order, with Lottie leading them directly towards the south. Long could they hear the old merman and his family calling after them words of good cheer, but gradually the sounds died away in the distance.

For some time they swam without speaking. Lottie moved along much faster than he ever had before, and Dollie found that it took all her energy and attention not to fall behind. However, like other little girls, she could not keep still very long, and after, as it seemed to her, they had covered many miles, she began to talk to her beloved Miss Martha.

"There's another poem I know about a whale," said she. "It's in my reader in school. Don't you remember it?

> " 'His angle-rod made of a sturdy oak;
>   His line a cable which in storm ne'er broke;
>   His hook he baited with a dragon's tail,
>   And sat upon a rock and bobbed for whale.' "

"That's the way a giant caught a whale," she explained. "Not that I'd want to try, even if I had such a big pole and line; I'm 'fraid he'd swim away with me; but the jingle runs through my head same as that one did through the Lieutenant's. Oh, I believe I'm getting a little tired. Don't you think we're most there?"

Her question did not need an answer in words. As she spoke, a mammoth form lifted itself from the depths below them. So close to them did it stop that she could reach forth her hand and touch its side. An instant later the sound of escaping water was heard, and the face of the ocean was splashed and spattered as though from a fountain. The whale had come to meet them.

Now that the tourists actually had found the object of their search, they scarcely knew how to proceed. It looked as big as a barn and as long as a railroad train. Something must be done; in a hurry, too, because at any moment it might dive and come up so far away that it could not be located.

"Speak to it, Sir Owl," whispered Dollie.

"You always make the speeches, you know."

"I'm willing enough to talk," he replied, "but this thing is so stretched out that for the life of me I can't tell which way to go to reach its ears."

Help in this dilemma came unexpectedly. All this time the whale had been watching them from his little eyes, set far back in his head. Now he inquired, gruffly: "What are you staring at me for? Think you're in the menagerie of a circus? Guess you never saw an animal as huge as I am, even there. Don't you know I could crush you with one sweep of my tail? Who are you, anyway?"

Sir Owl politely went through the customary form of telling about his companions and himself, and of the objects for which they were searching.

"Well," replied the whale, sullenly, "you needn't expect any help from me; and I'd like to see you try and take a bone from *my* head. You're a queer outfit, and I don't want anything to do with you. Let me alone; it's my night to be cross, and when I'm cross, I'm ugly."

Here indeed was a crisis. Neither the brave Lieutenant nor the wise owl seemed to know what to do. The whale was too powerful to be attacked, and in too bad a humor to grant a favor. While the others hesitated, Miss Martha drew Ann to one side and whispered to her earnestly.

The conversation apparently amused the cat-ghost. With a grin on her sharp face, she swam out directly in front of the animal's head and tauntingly sang the following verse:

> "There was a mighty whale
> Who had a lengthy tail
> Extending 'way back from his forehead;
> And when he was good
> He was very, very good,
> But when he was bad he was horrid."

"What's that?" roared he. "Who's making sport of me? It's that cat thing, is it? I gave her fair warning. Now I'm going to swallow her whole."

"Come along," challenged Ann.

Immediately he made a mad rush and opened his big jaws like a cellar-door. An instant later they closed over Ann, who never moved. Lottie

gave a sob of grief, and even the others trembled for the safety of their rash friend—all except Sir Owl.

"That's the time she went too far," cried he.
"Good riddance. I never knew a cat who
amounted to anything except to make a noise.
Now we can have some peace."

This seemed also to be the opinion of the
whale. "She went down so easily I couldn't
feel her," quoth he. "Have you any more? I'm
still hungry."

"There's one right close to you," replied Miss
Martha, pointing towards Ann, who a second
time had stationed herself opposite him. Of
course she had not been swallowed at all, but,
ghost-like, had slipped out through his body.

Again Ann sang to him, teasingly:

> "Cross-patch,
> Can't catch
>   A spirit quick as I;
> When you have done
> You've bit your tongue,
>   And I have passed you by."

"Another songster," cried he. "Good! Here's
at her!" But this time Ann led him a long

chase before she was overtaken; and the opera-
tion was repeated at least a dozen times ere he
realized that he was being made the victim of
a joke.

When this idea was confirmed by Ann's jeers
and laughter, his chagrin was so great that, with
one snort of rage, he dashed madly away and
soon disappeared from view.

"Now, isn't that too bad?" sobbed Dollie.
"There he goes, bones and all. Wherever shall
we find another? I'm most ready to cry."

"Better laugh instead," said Ann, who had
just returned from the chase. "What do you
suppose this thing in my mouth is?"

"It looks so funny," exclaimed the curious
child, taking the object in her hands. "It's
black, and bends back and forth like whalebone.
Why, it is whalebone. Oh, goody, goody! Now,
we've three things for the broth. But however
did you find it?"

"Perhaps I can tell better than anyone else,"
said Miss Martha. "You know our natural history says that whalebone grows in the monster's
upper jaw. As he would not give us any, it oc-

curred to me that if Ann went inside she might find a loose piece which she could tear off and carry away. The rest of the scheme she worked out herself, so you must not praise me too much. But perhaps Sir Owl at last will admit that it does one good to study books."

The big bird evidently had been somewhat perplexed. Now his eyes brightened as he remarked, in a superior manner: "I have always admitted the value of books, and I always have said that a wise person scorns no aid, however humble. In the task before us, there are minor details I am glad to have worked out by you and the others. But let me ask you, who first proposed the visit to the cloud? I, Sir Oliver Owl. Who has counselled you and advised you and cared for you, from the oak-tree to this very point? I, Sir Oliver Owl. Without me there would have been no expedition. You may win praise as my companions, but mine will be the chief glory. Everywhere I shall be known as the mighty slayer of the Magical Man of Mirth. To who; to who-o!"

"And, pray, what about me?" asked Lieutenant Lobster, peevishly. "That's what I want to know. Who furnished the linament? Who took you to the wreck? Who led the fight against the serpent? What would an army be without its commander?"

"Do stop your quar'ling," Dollie pleaded. "I'm sure there's 'nough for us all to do, and we ought to be a very happy fam'ly. See, we've the nail, the fin and the bone. Now we want the shell, 'cause it won't do any good to find the black water 'less we have something to put it in. Let's go up to the very top and p'raps we can see the lady turtle the merman told us 'bout. Come ahead."

And in the thought of the work to be done, the differences of the moment were forgotten.

CHAPTER VIII

EGGS AND A SHELL

CHAPTER VIII

EGGS AND A SHELL

When Dollie reached the surface, she bobbed her head into the air and took several deep breaths, which gave her fresh strength and vigor. Her example was followed by Sir Oliver, who at once tooted loudly as though he also were pleased with the brief change. The others remained just below; and so all swam leisurely along, in hopes that they soon would come across Mrs. Turtle, or someone else who could help them in their mission.

When in the hollows between the waves, the two sentinels could see only a short distance, but while borne upward on the crests, their bright eyes commanded a broad view in all directions. Nevertheless, for quite a time nothing of interest could be descried. Then, all of a sudden, a strange spot on the water attracted Dollie's attention.

"There's something big and round and dark

floating south of us," she cried, in a moment. "Let's go see what it is. Looks to me like an old wash-tub."

"For sometime I have been watching it," said Sir Owl, whose glowing orbs had been sweeping the sea like search-lights. "Nothing ever escapes the keenness of my vision. But who ever heard of a wash-tub in such a place? In my judgment I have discovered a crow's nest. Cats; serpents; crows! Am I never to escape from these creatures of evil habits? Let me tear this nest to pieces so that no longer it may be a refuge for such hateful beings."

This remark aroused Miss Martha's mirth. "Do you suppose crows build their homes in the middle of the ocean?" she asked. "If you'd read some of my books, you'd know more than you do now, or I'm much mistaken."

While this dispute was going on, all had been moving rapidly towards the point Dollie had indicated; and now Lottie, who, as scout, had darted ahead of the rest, returned with his report.

"You're both wrong," he shouted, a-tremble

with eagerness. "'Tisn't a wash-tub nor a bird's nest. It's a lady turtle, that's what it is, and I'll bet she's the very one that merman spoke about. My, but she's a whopper; and she's sound asleep!"

His words proved true; and soon all gathered around a gigantic form that was swashing up and down on the ocean swells, while its huge flippers hung limp and apparently lifeless.

"I must awaken her," remarked Sir Owl, "and then converse with her. She will be pleased to meet a bird of my wisdom."

So speaking, he thrust his beak up against the end of her shell, into which she had withdrawn her head when she prepared for her nap, and shrieked his loudest.

"What's the matter?" mumbled a sleepy voice from within.

"I wish to talk with you; I, Oliver Owl."

"Buy cod liver oil?" repeated the voice drowsily. "No, I don't want any. Peddlers are not allowed around these premises, either." And no further reply could be elicited, though the owl hooted frantically again and again.

"Let me try," advised the Lieutenant. "Often the warrior is more powerful than the sage."

Deftly he poked one of his claws into the opening and nipped Mrs. Turtle sharply on the end of her nose.

This action had the desired effect. Out popped her head, with a spring like that of a jack-in-the box. Still stupid with sleep, she blinked her eyes and yawned.

"What do you mean by waking me up in that manner?" she scolded. "I told you once I don't need any oil. I'm fat enough already."

"Oil, oil!" shouted Sir Owl, who was angered that he should be taken for a peddler. "I said that I am Sir Oliver Owl, the wisest bird in the whole universe. I desire you to tell me where I can find a shell——"

"Take that lobster's," interrupted Mrs. Turtle. "Sakes alive! You don't expect me to give you mine? And cold weather coming on so soon! But I haven't time to argue with you. Lucky you woke me up, or I might have missed a most important engagement. Good-bye."

Even before she had finished speaking, her

great flippers began to churn the water, like the screws of a steam launch, and she was well under way ere her sudden action was realized by anyone but Lieutenant Lobster. That experienced soldier, however, was not to be taken unawares.

"Halt! halt!" he commanded, in his sternest tones; and when not the slightest heed was paid to his orders, he extended a claw and grabbed Mrs. Turtle savagely by the tip of her tail. Perhaps her skin was so thick and horny that she did not feel him. At any rate, she did not slacken speed, but forged swiftly ahead, while he hung grimly on behind.

Dollie was inclined to laugh at this strange sight, but she quickly recollected that this was no matter of fun. Mrs. Turtle probably was headed towards the island where could be found the shell without a crack, and even if she were not, the Lieutenant must not be deserted. So, saving her breath, she started in quick pursuit, in which she was joined by Sir Oliver, Miss Martha, Ann and Lottie.

The chase turned out to be a severe one. Mrs.

Turtle evidently knew where she was going. As evidently, she intended to reach the desired spot at the earliest possible moment, without waiting for anyone else. The Lieutenant, fast to her tail, had no trouble in keeping up; Lottie, Ann and Miss Martha were able to glide through the water without any apparent effort; but Sir Oliver and Dollie, who swam by main strength, found the necessary speed most exhausting.

The bird began to puff and blow, as though his lungs could not obtain enough air, and Dollie's arms and legs commenced to ache all over. It is a wonder that neither gave up or even complained, and it is to the credit of all that there was not a single straggler when Mrs. Turtle finally slackened speed in the shallows close to the shore of a small island, which unexpectedly rose out of the sea in front of them.

Here the Lieutenant released his hold and again tried to talk to Mrs. Turtle, but to no avail. When she no longer could swim, she commenced to crawl. So far she had not paid the slightest attention to those who had followed her; but, as she climbed upon the beach, she called back, "I've something that will keep me busy as can be for a while. Don't any of you dare to come up here and disturb me. Let me alone, and when I return I'll tell you what I've been doing."

"It is my duty to accompany her," stated Sir Owl, as soon as she had disappeared from view. "You may be sure she is up to some mischief or other. She reminds me of a cat, except that she has a shell instead of hair."

"Yes," retorted Miss Martha, "everything is like everything else except where it is different. How wise you are! But you forget what we are seeking. I vow, nothing would be done if we trusted to you. Pray, why did we follow Mrs. Turtle?"

"To find a shell," interrupted Ann and Lottie at the same time. "We've been looking around already, and we haven't seen a single one."

Dollie and the others now joined in the search. They walked and they crawled and they swam in all directions; they poked and they clawed and they scratched in the sand; but, in deep water or in shallow, behind rocks or out in the open, the result always was the same. Not a shell of any kind could be found.

"Oh, dear me," sighed Dollie, "it's no use to try any more. The merman certainly didn't know what he was talking 'bout."

"That cat is to be blamed for it," asserted Sir Owl. "I knew all the time that she would spoil everything. The ship captain was right. She's a hoodoo and not a mascot. Now let her leave us, or I'll make her into the ghost of a ghost. In spite of her, I shall discover the shell!"

"You shouldn't scold in the presence of ladies," remarked the pleasant voice of Mrs. Turtle, who, unnoticed in the excitement, had again taken her place beside them. "No one knows the ocean as well as the old merman, and whatever he told you must be true; so Ann cannot be at fault. But, speaking of shells, I've just laid twelve dozen eggs up there on the shore. Now, what do you say to that?" And she smiled complacently.

"Mercy!" cried Dollie, for the moment unmindful of anything else. "Twelve dozen! Why don't you put 'em in a basket and carry 'em to a hotel? You could get fifty cents a dozen for 'em, easy."

Mrs. Turtle drew herself up proudly. "My eggs are my children," she answered, "and it is not my custom to sell my family. I suppose there are plenty of humans, though, and especially little girls, who would be glad to eat them," she added, glancing directly at Dollie.

"Oh, I didn't mean what I said," cried the embarrassed child; "I was thinking of hens. You know they lay all the time and don't miss a few now and then. Won't you forgive me?"

"No offense in the least," Mrs. Turtle assured her. "I don't know any hens and don't wish to."

"But tell me about your nest," requested Dollie, anxious to change the subject. "Is it built of sticks, and are you going back to sit on it?"

"Sticks, indeed!" Mrs. Turtle was not yet more than half pacified. "That's a pretty idea. I might as well learn to climb a tree and make a house like a bird. My nest is scooped out of the soft, clean sand, and my eggs are covered with the same warm stuff."

"You might with profit take lessons from a wise bird like me," interrupted Sir Owl. "Locate your next home in a hollow tree, where it is always dry and cozy. Close to the opening there should be a limb whereon you can sit and meditate."

"I'm sure you're all right just as you are," continued Dollie, without giving the owl a chance to say more. "But do you go back and sit on the eggs?"

"What in the world should I sit on them for? Haven't I mashed two shells already? Would you have me crush the rest? I never saw such a murderous and bloodthirsty being!"

Dollie was growing confused. Her every remark, however innocent, simply made matters worse.

"Won't you excuse me?" she pleaded. "I was thinking of hens again. Of course, you aren't at all alike, and I'd forgotten about your being so heavy. Would you mind telling me what does hatch out the little turtles?"

"The heat of the sun."

"And you wait here till tnat's done, and then

hurry to take care of your babies. How jolly!"

Once more Dollie was guessing poorly. "Nothing of the kind," corrected Mrs. Turtle. "When my offspring are born, I shall be hundreds of miles away. Let them take care of themselves, as I did."

Dollie was so vexed with herself that she almost cried. This immediately softened Mrs. Turtle's heart.

"Don't feel badly, my girl," she whispered kindly. "Perhaps I've been cross, but you must overlook it. All humans and animals have habits and customs different from each other. No wonder you mix me up with a hen. But let me ask *you* some questions. What is that shell you folks were chatting about as I came up? And what are you doing down here, anyway?"

"We're after a wicked magician, the Magical Man of Mirth," answered Dollie, glad to go back to the subject that was nearest her heart. "See, I've a rusty nail and a piece of porpoise's fin. Next we need a shell to put 'em in, black water to fill it with, and hot water to boil 'em over. Then we give the drink to the Magical

Man and, bing! he's dead in a minute."

"So that's it," mused the turtle; "and the mer-man said you'd find the right shell here, did he? Now, just what did he mean? There are sea-shells and river-shells, nut-shells and egg-shells, bomb-shells and gun-shells, and—why, I do be-lieve I found what you want while I was dig-ging my nest. Wait a moment."

Clumsily she flopped and splashed onto the shore and quickly she flopped and splashed back again, to deposit at Dollie's feet a small, glisten-ing tube, closed at one end and open at the other.

"Why, it's a brass gun-shell, just like one of brother Bob's," exclaimed Dollie, as she grabbed up her treasures. "You couldn't ever crack it. I do b'lieve it's the very thing. See," she continued hurriedly, "I roll the piece of por-poise's fin up, and it just fits inside. Next, the rusty nail goes in this way. It doesn't quite reach the edge, so it'll hold up the round pebble that I'll put on top of it. Then, when we find the black water, I'll pack clay 'round the pebble so the water won't leak out. Isn't it perfectly lovely?" Her question was addressed to Miss Martha, but it was Sir Owl who answered.

"Of course, everything is all right," quoth he. "I know shells like that and they contain a most potent magic. Once, when I was sitting on a limb beside my wife, discoursing to her on the thisness of the thus, a boy nearby put one of those tubes into a hollow stick and pointed it at us. There was a terrible roar, and my wife fell from the perch and broke her neck. Through my leadership you have discovered the means to destroy the Magical Man of Mirth. What a great bird am I!"

"You certainly make a great noise," admitted Miss Martha.

"And I am glad I have been able to help Dollie and the rest of you," said Mrs. Turtle. "But, my dear child, did not the merman warn you not to proceed with the adventure? I'm sure he did. The black water can best be obtained at the bottom of the ocean, where lurk all kinds of horrible and dangerous monsters. The only hot spring is said to be far away to the south, where the surrounding ocean is too cold for comfort.

And, when you have all the stuff, how ever are you to get it down the throat of the fierce magician? Take the advice of an old lady, and give up this wild idea."

"Excuse me for interrupting," interposed Miss Martha, "but Dollie is in my care, and I'm older than you are. We can't quit now, and it won't do any good to try to scare us. That's settled."

"Well, if you will, you will," responded Mrs. Turtle, "and good luck to you. When you start for the hot water, see if you can't find the home of the seals and have a talk with their king. He knows all about the icy regions and like as not has bathed in the spring itself. Now I must leave."

"Wait a jiffy," cried Lottie. "Let *me* ask a question. S'pose someone cut off your head early in the morning. Couldn't you and wouldn't you die till after sunset?"

"You odd little rascal," laughed she. "How can I tell now? Wait till someone lops off my head. Then perhaps I'll come back and let you know what happens. Farewell!"

Once more her huge flippers churned the sea

as she dashed away. This time Dollie and her companions did not exert themselves to keep up with her. Instead, they started slowly and thoughtfully. In Dollie's pocket safely reposed the shell with the rusty nail and the porpoise's fin. So far, so good; but what might not happen ere they secured the other objects of their search, and what would be the result of their final contest with the Magical Man of Mirth?

CHAPTER IX

DOLLIE IN DISTRESS

CHAPTER IX

DOLLIE IN DISTRESS

After the march towards the south had been kept up for some time, Sir Owl could be heard softly whistling to himself.

"Whatever are you making that silly noise for?" asked Miss Martha, sharply.

"I am imitating the playing of a flute," replied he. "Don't you remember the beautiful poem about the tutor who tooted a flute? Wait, and I will recite it to you."

"You'll do nothing of the kind. You can toot your flute or flute your toot around here forever, if you want to. The rest of us have something better to do, and it begins to look as though I'll have to boss the job. Lottie, isn't the ocean about as deep here as it is anywhere?"

"Yes'm," replied the guide. "I was just going to say——"

"Never mind what you were going to say. Just watch what I do." With these words, she

147

dropped to the bottom like a stone.

Lottie, not to be outdone, assumed a position so that his tail pointed towards the sky and dived after her. The others, not hesitating an instant, did the same. Soon, without a single mishap, all landed on the top of a plateau arising from the true floor of the sea.

This table-land, on which they now rested, was exceedingly rough, and was covered with slabs of rock, loose boulders and sharp stones. The sand and earth had been washed out from the crevices, so that little canyons, five or ten feet deep, ran here and there and joined or branched off from one another in bewildering confusion. There were numerous caves and caverns, too, of various sizes, where the water had worked under from below.

The Lieutenant, who had planned many a shrewd campaign, was quick to grasp the advantages of the situation. "It's the very place," cried he. "In those canyons and caverns must lie the things we seek. That we may cover the whole ground rapidly, let us separate and each make careful search. Then we can return and compare notes as to what we have discovered."

This was agreeable to all, except that Dollie and Miss Martha decided to keep together. They were too dear friends to be parted, even for a brief period. Dollie still carried her dagger, thrust through her sash, so that she felt fully able to protect both her friend and herself from the attack of any hidden enemy.

In the beginning, the two walked side by side, and, keeping close together, they carefully watched every bend, or passage from one rift to another. However, their interest in the many things they came across soon made them careless, and they proceeded Indian file, Dollie ahead.

Scattered around them were beautiful shells and pebbles. Tiny, gaily-colored animals, like crabs or lizards, darted about close to their holes in the plateau; fishes, strange in shape, time and again almost bumped into the explorers, and then dashed away in alarm. Everywhere was something odd and new.

No wonder the two soon drifted apart, for one object attracted one, and another the other. Dollie, who still was in the lead, came to where the way forked. She went to the left, and called to Miss Martha that she had done so. The latter did not hear her and took the road to the right. Then the defiles split again, and in a few moments the wanderers, all unconscious of what had happened, were widely separated.

When Miss Martha did realize that she was alone, and that Dollie was not near her, she became frantic. Over and over, loud and long, she called the child's name; but there was no response. Quickly she poised herself in the water above the walls and gazed anxiously in all directions; nowhere could Dollie be seen. Hurrying to where she thought the first division in the trail had occurred, she traced the other branch; but the more she sought, the more confused she became. At last she gave up, and, sitting down, began to weep bitterly.

"What's the matter?" the well-known voice of Lieutenant Lobster shouted in her ear. "Have you fallen down and cracked yourself?"

"Not at all," sobbed she, "and it isn't any joke. Dollie's lost, and I can't find her."

"Nonsense," said the Lieutenant. "If you

missed each other, she's returned to the starting-place. Come with me; she'll be there, laughing at you."

"I don't believe it. I, myself, couldn't make out the way back, and she can't, either."

But the Lieutenant insisted, and was forced to admit that he was wrong. They reached the spot where they had landed; Lottie and Sir Oliver were on hand, but not Dollie. Ann also was missing.

When informed of the trouble, Lottie was overwhelmed with grief. "You folks stay right here," he screamed excitedly. "I'll scout around these canyons. If Dollie's in any one of 'em, I'll bring her back in a jiffy. When Ann returns, you let her know what's wrong. She can help. She's a mighty bright ghost, I want to tell you."

Lottie was so nervous that it was time for someone of force and decision to take charge. As might be expected, the Lieutenant rose to the occasion.

"Miss Martha, stop your crying," he ordered. "You can do that after we've found Dollie. Lottie, stand still and quiet your nerves. Now

listen to me.   We'll hunt together.   Lottie can
guide, as he's used to it, but I must be along to
plan, and Sir Oliver to counsel.   No need for
anyone to wait here.   If the dear girl could come,
she'd be with us now.   As for Ann, if she has a
ghostly gift, she will seek us as quickly else-
where.   But I agree with Sir Owl; you can't
rely much on cat-spooks when it comes down to
business.   Miss Martha, you must show Lottie
as nearly as you can what route you took.   Forward,   march!"

The Lieutenant, in order that he might command a broad view, clung to the feathers on Sir
Oliver's back, and managed to crouch securely
in that position.   Thus the four, Lottie in advance, wound in and out among the rifts in the
table-land.

The prospect was discouraging.   All places
looked so much alike that Miss Martha's mem-
ory was of small help.   Every few steps she
shouted Dollie's name, but there was no reply.
Though all desired to keep up the search, it
really seemed that they were not on the right
track.   Finally the Lieutenant hopped to a ledge

NOT TEN FEET BELOW SAT DOLLIE, APPARENTLY SAFE AND SOUND

nearby and asked the others to gather around
him for a conference.

The place upon which they rested was only a
few yards wide and divided one hollow from the
next. While the Lieutenant and Sir Owl were
deep in their discussion, Miss Martha crawled
across and peeped over the opposite side. What
a surprise! Not ten feet below, with her back
against the rocky wall, sat Dollie, apparently
safe and sound.

"Dollie, Dollie!" called she, leaning over.
"Are you hurt? And why didn't you answer
when I called?"

How quickly Dollie heard, and how quickly
she lifted her grief-lined face! "Oh, Miss Martha, dear," she whispered, "I'm so glad you've
come. I knew you would. Some mean old thing
in the cave behind that big slab over there, has
tied ropes to my feet, so I can't move. He says
he's going to pull me inside and eat me up if I
make a noise. Help, me, quick!"

"I'll have the Lieutenant jump down and snip
the ropes with his pinchers," cried Miss Martha.
"Then you can swim away."

"Slowly, slowly," advised the Lieutenant, who had crossed over to see what had happened. "There may be a lot more of those feelers that Dollie calls ropes—more than I could nip before they had me fast, too. Let me first talk to the hidden monster."

Then, in his most military tone, he demanded: "Who are you, and what do you mean by binding this girl?"

"Who are you, and what do you mean by asking me such questions?" came the surly answer.

"I am Sir Oliver Owl," interrupted the bird, who felt that it was time for him to take a hand. "I am the wisest being in the universe, and you will release that child at once or suffer my wrath."

"What do I care?" was the gruff response. "That stone has slipped down and stopped up the mouth of my cave so that I can't get anything but my legs out. I'm starving to death, anyway."

"I'll tell you," suggested Miss Martha, "untie her, and we'll tip the rock over and turn you loose. Isn't that fair?"

For an instant there was silence. Then, the bonds slipped from Dollie's ankles and disappeared. She was free; and instantly she darted upward to clasp Miss Martha in her arms. The Lieutenant rubbed his claws softly against her gown, and even Sir Owl caressed her with his beak. Lottie, in his joy, swam circles with such speed as almost to make one dizzy.

But it was necessary to fulfill Miss Martha's promise. So Dollie, looking around, picked up a thick iron rod that must have fallen from some passing ship. By using this as a lever and exerting all her strength, she managed to topple over the slab that blocked the entrance to the den. Whoever or whatever was inside, now could appear.

The curiosity of all was at once satisfied. From the cave there backed what at first resembled a half-filled gunny-sack. Extending in all directions from around its opening were ten long streamers, which Dollie had called ropes. As it turned and faced the wondering group, they could see a horrid, gaping mouth in the center of a mass of wriggling legs; and behind this mouth two large, black, unwinking eyes, possessing a most wicked glare.

"Why, you're a devil-fish, aren't you?" cried Miss Martha. "Your picture's in our natural history, only there you're sitting up like a flower-pot, and here you're spread around."

"So, you have just discovered that, have you, my book-loving Miss Martha?" asked Sir Oliver, condescendingly. "I could have told you long ago, but I think it strengthens your mind to let you work things out for yourself."

"My mind's strong enough as it is," snapped Miss Martha. "And if you would tell some of these things before, instead of after they happened, I'd have more faith in your wisdom. But what's the matter with Lottie? He looks as if he had an idea."

"Why didn't that big devil-fish push the door open from the inside? Queer, isn't it? Could if I were big as he is."

"But not if you were what I am. I could pull this whole mountain down if my legs were long enough to reach around it; but how, please, can I push with such wobbly things? And I can't go straight ahead, either; when I want to move frontwards, I have to turn around and go backwards."

While Lottie puzzled over this explanation, Dollie inquired how the cave came to be stopped up.

The devil-fish wiped his eyes with the ends of his legs, as he answered mournfully, "I'm always in trouble because I'm so sweet and soft—just like a chocolate-drop. All the big fishes try to eat me, and I have to hide under the rocks to escape them. Well, a fierce monster dived after me, knocked me over a stone, and locked me in the hole. But you watch me. I'll fix him next trip! and I do believe he's coming now. Conceal yourselves somewhere, instantly."

Lieutenant Lobster rolled into a convenient crevice. Lottie darted off at top speed. Miss Martha, Sir Owl and Dollie jumped behind a boulder whence they could peek out and see what happened. As they did so, a dark shadow covered them, and some immense animal swept by so fast that they could feel the rush of water following in its wake.

Describing a graceful curve, it shot far towards the surface, turned, and made another terrific descent. This time its body brushed the ground before the devil-fish's place of abode. He, fearing that he might be discovered, made use of a strange power such creatures possess and discolored the surrounding ocean as though by upsetting a barrel of black ink.

Sir Oliver, to his credit, was the first to notice the presence of the black water. "Hurry, hurry!" he screamed, flapping his wings and ruffling his feathers in his eagerness. "I told you all the time, I, the wise owl, would find it. Fill your shell before it floats away. Quick, quick!"

Before he had finished this harangue, Dollie had dashed forth. She was entirely unmindful of the fact that the attacking animal might dive down again and gobble her up, instead of the devil-fish. Into her left hand she dropped the pebble, and with her right she swung the shell containing the rusty nail and the porpoise's fin, back and forth through the discolored ocean. Next she replaced the pebble and deftly plastered over and around it a handful of sticky clay, found near the boulder behind which she had been hiding. Then she rejoined Sir Owl, whose flapping wings and bristling feathers still showed his interest in what was going on.

Nor too soon did she regain her place of safety. A second later, with rush and swirl, the fight was renewed; and this time came the desired opportunity. As the foe again flashed in front of the hiding-place, the devil-fish made a flying leap and landed, fairly and squarely, on its back, close to its head. His ten long legs he wrapped and twined around its mouth and jaws; thus was his revenge complete.

There followed a deadly struggle, which all watched with bulging eyes. The fish rolled in the sand, rubbed against the cliffs, and by a dozen different methods tried to get rid of its rider; but in vain. Securely he kept his place, as does the cowboy who sticks to his saddle on a bucking broncho.

What the end was none of the party ever knew. Suddenly the beast with its burden dashed towards the surface, while the devil-fish, releasing one leg, waved it in fond adieu. That was the last seen or heard of either of them.

"Good riddance," quoth Lieutenant Lobster, who now crawled forth again.

"And I agree with you," declared Miss Martha. "That satanic fish is the slimiest, wriggliest thing I ever saw. But gracious! Here's Lottie. He came back so swiftly he almost scared me. Now, where in the world is Ann?"

"She has left us," announced Sir Owl. "Of that you may be sure. Have I not told you that all cats are cowards? The danger which I have met, she feared. The peril which I have encountered drove her from us in alarm. But be of good cheer. Her absence means good luck. Did I not obtain the black water as soon as she departed? As long as you have the benefit of my wisdom, naught else is necessary. Think no more of Ann, and give thanks to Sir Owl."

"Of course we thank you," cried Dollie. "Now we have all the things to make the broth out of and they're corked up tight in the shell in my pocket. But we'd all breathe better if we'd go up top again. It's so dark and cellary down here I feel creepy."

The ascent was made in safety and without delay; but a fresh surprise was in store for the adventurers. As soon as Dollie and Sir Owl stuck their heads above the surface, right in front of them they beheld a mighty ship, with all sails set; and, wonder of wonders, over her side was thrust a misty face which meowed a most familiar greeting.

Ann was found; but what could she be doing on board a boat?

CHAPTER X

ENTRAPPED BY SEALS

CHAPTER X

"Hello, Ann," called Lottie, when he beheld his friend leaning over the vessel's side. "Any fun up there? Come on down and see a fellow."

"You are under arrest as a deserter," thundered the Lieutenant. "Appear before me at once for trial. If guilty, you shall be shot at sunrise."

"And it will give me great pleasure to witness the event," added Sir Owl. "At length you have been found out and soon you will meet the fate you deserve."

At first Ann's only answer was a series of yowls, in which Dollie thought she could detect a note of triumph. Then, nervously switching her tail a few times, as any cat does before she leaps, she sprang through the air and alighted in the midst of her companions.

"Some of you don't seem very glad to welcome

165

me back," she announced calmly, "though I reckon you'd have hard work shooting a ghost; but wait till you hear my story. , That ugly bird with the yellow eyes has been taunting me ever since we met. I've been looking for a chance to show him that I'm no fool. So, when down below I sensed this approaching ship, I came up. And what do you think I've found on board her? A big kettle of boiling hot water in the galley. The cook's fast asleep, too, and no one else about. Now go ahead and finish your broth. It will be lots easier than hunting around in the ocean. What do you think of that?"

"Lots easier," sneered Sir Oliver Owl. "That's just like a cat. Can Dollie or Miss Martha or Lottie or the Lieutenant climb up on that ship? Of course not. You and I are the only ones who are able to leave the water. Ladies first, always, my dear madam. Take the shell, seek the galley, boil your broth, and good luck to you. Only look out and don't get nailed up in a picture again. I should be so sorry to lose you."

"It's you who are the coward," retorted Ann,

savagely. "I've found the water. That's my part. You fly up and make the stew. That's your part. You well know I can't hold the shell in my ghost of a paw!"

"Let me be heard," said the Lieutenant. "Ann has done well. She is acquitted of the charge of desertion and restored to full rank in the army. But the task she points out is one of great peril and who should incur this if not I, your commander? Dollie, place the shell in one of my claws. Sir Oliver, bear me on your back to the railing. There, in safety, you can remain on guard while I boil the broth, or perish in the attempt."

"Do you really and truly think you're going to be caught?" asked Dollie. "P'raps you'd better not go at all. You're such a nice old lobster, and I just couldn't stand it to have you get hurt."

"It is no sign of cowardice when a soldier admits the hazard of his task," replied the Lieutenant. "Doubtless I can reach the galley in safety. But what if the cook awakes while I am there? Then shall I be placed in the pot and boiled alive. In that case, in truth shall I make the broth, but it will be with my own body, and for the captain's dinner. Nevertheless I go. If I return not, remember me kindly."

Without another word he took the shell from Dollie's outstretched hand and perched himself on the back of Sir Owl, who, shaking the water from his wings, soared upward and alighted on the stern of the ship. Immediately the Lieutenant could be seen, springing swiftly to the deck, whereupon he disappeared from view.

Dollie cuddled Miss Martha in her arms, as she loved to do when sorry or lonesome, and Lottie snuggled up close to her gown. Anxiously they gazed into the night, meanwhile moving along to keep pace with the boat as it drifted slowly in the faint breeze. Hard they strained their ears to catch the faintest sound which might give them a clue to the fate in store for their heroic leader. Nor did they even notice that Ann had left them.

Nothing could be heard but the flapping of a sail, the creaking of a rope, or the lapping of a wave against the vessel's hull. Merrily twinkled the stars; softly blew the cool night breeze; gently rose and fell the wavelets, to rise and fall again. Everything seemed to speak of calm and peace, yet somewhere in that calm and peace the brave Lieutenant, alone and unaided, was slowly crawling to what might be his cruel fate.

The strain was almost more than Dollie, in the kindness of her heart, could bear, and she was about to scream or cry—which, she was not sure—when something happened, or rather a multitude of things happened. First, the dead silence was broken by the gleeful shout of a man; then came a succession of yowls from Ann; a series of wild toots from Sir Oliver; a crash of pans, pots and dishes falling on hard planks; orders, sharp and loud, from some officer; and the tramp of many feet, as the sailors rushed to obey.

In the midst of the din, Lieutenant Lobster, Ann and Sir Oliver appeared at the ship's rim and plunged headlong into the sea. The pallor on the Lieutenant's face and the trembling of his claws showed that he had been in deadly danger; the absence of a handful of Sir Owl's tail feathers was proof that he, too, had been in the thick of the fight; but Ann showed no signs of wear or tear. **On the contrary, she began to purr contentedly.**

With forced calmness, the Lieutenant made explanation, as soon as he recovered his breath. "This has been the wildest adventure of my long life," he announced, "and that I am restored to you alive and uninjured, I am proud to acknowledge, is due to the boldness of our true friends, Ann and Sir Oliver Owl.

"After gaining the deck, I worked my way unnoticed to the galley. There, as Ann had said, stood the pot of boiling water. There, too, sat the cook, fast asleep. By the side of the pot was a small box, upon which I clambered so that I might dip the shell in the scalding liquid. So far, all was well. But here the man awoke and fixed his staring eyes upon me. Then, indeed, I thought that all was over.

"Shiver me timbers," cried he, in his sailor's lingo, "if there isn't a lobster trying to make soup of himself. Wait till I help you, my beauty." And, rising, he stretched forth a hairy arm. But he reckoned without counting the other members of my band.

"From out the darkness sailed Ann, like a crazy bat. Right on his head she landed. Her howls and the scratches from her clammy paws caused him to scream with fright. A second later, appeared Sir Owl, who through the open door had spied my danger. With glaring eyes, open beak, and whisking wings, straight into the cook's face dashed he. The first scratch from his talons drew blood. Reeling backward from this double attack, my enemy toppled over the rack on which were set his dishes. Above—hoots and yowls and yells; below—the crash of pots and pans and plates! Is it strange that the officer of the deck called out the watch and that in the confusion we three escaped? Again I offer thanks to my rescuers. Dollie, here is your shell. I return unsuccessful, but I trust not dishonored."

"'Course you're not dishonored," exclaimed Dollie, putting the treasured shell again in her pocket. "You're a hero, just like we read about in books. If I had my little gold cross here, I'd give it to you and pin it on your breast."

"You should pin it on mine," insisted Sir Owl. "On mine, I say! Who came to his relief? I, Sir Oliver Owl. To whom does he owe his life? To me, Sir Oliver Owl. Am I not the bravest of the brave, as well as the wisest of the wise?"

"But there is a graver matter to talk about," he screamed, with increasing wrath. "Who concocted the vile plot? Ann, the cat ghost! Who has caused me to lose half of my glorious tail feathers? Ann, the treacherous, traitorous cat ghost! How long must I warn you against her? Let her be hanged at sunset, chopped into mince-meat at midnight, and shot at sunrise!"

"Do be still," urged Miss Martha. "Your squalling makes my ears ring. Ann is all right. You wanted hot water, and she found it for you. Don't blame her because you got *into hot water*. You ought to be proud that you helped rescue your friends, and don't forget that Ann did as much as you did. Let us be calm and decent."

"And 'member what a big story you have to

tell at the next meeting of the Omnip'tent Owls, or whatever you call 'em," cried Dollie. " 'Twouldn't s'prise me the least bit if they named a school-house after you, and raised your sal'ry. Wouldn't that be fine?"

This suggestion pleased the bird so that he scolded no more, and instead commenced to preen his rumpled feathers. As to Ann, she seemed entirely careless of what anyone said about her or threatened to do to her. Plainly she knew her own business and felt able to take care of herself.

"Well," said the Lieutenant, who now had recovered his good spirits, "while we have been talking, the ship has sailed away. Let her go— and let us again take up the march. A good commander best displays his skill and courage in the time of defeat. Both the merman and Mrs. Turtle referred to a boiling spring far towards the south. Then, to the south let us go. Lottie, guide on. Forward, march."

One might suppose that by this time Dollie would have become tired or disheartened. However, such a person would be very much mis-

taken. It is true that her search for the broth
and then for the Magical Man of Mirth was
taking longer than she had expected, but, as all
her friends know, she is a plucky and determined
child, and the harder the task the more she felt
bound to pursue it. Though she was disap-
pointed at the failure of the sortie upon the
ship, the shell, joggling around in her pocket,
reminded her that much had been done already,
and that what remained could be accomplished
also, if she did not give up.

Frequently, too, she thought of the poor, sad
Queen of the City of Mirth, who doubtless was
counting the moments till she and her cloud-
home should be restored to a state of joy and
comfort. The little bickerings among Dollie's
friends did not bother her at all. Rather was
she amused, because she well knew that, right
down in their hearts, they all loved one another,
and would stand by one another, as was shown by
the manner in which Sir Owl and Ann had
hastened to the aid of the Lieutenant.

With thoughts such as these, Dollie busied her
mind as they sped swiftly on their way. Her

companions also must have been visiting the land
of dreams, for, without the slightest warning,
they all bumped into a furry object that, unnoticed, had floated across their path. Sir Oliver,
as soon as he felt the hair, commenced his usual
tirade against cats, which was cut short by Dollie, who had a different idea.

"It isn't a kitty," she cried. "It's more like
seal-skin. Why, Miss Martha, it *is* seal-skin.
We'll take it home, won't we? There's plenty
for a muff for me, and a cap for Brother Bob.
Hurrah!"

"You'll take me home, will you?" This
question came in sweet tones from one end of
the object, where now could be seen a pair of
mild, dark eyes and a black, velvety nose.
"Then you'll slay me by striking me on the
head with a club, and with a sharp knife you'll
cut off my pretty covering, so that you can have
a beautiful cap and muff? Don't you humans
ever think of us, and whether we want to die?
I knew coarse, rough men did such things, but
I hoped little girls were more kind."

"Oh, I hadn't the slightest idea you were a

live seal," cried Dollie, who is as tender and loving a girl as ever lived. "I thought you were skinned already. Why didn't you speak sooner?"

"That makes no difference," said the seal. "You wear garments made from our pelts. If you didn't, no one would bother us. You encourage bad men to hunt us and to kill us cruelly. Oh, why don't you and your people understand? So happy are we in the sea and on the rocks! Isn't it pitiful that savage beings should come and slaughter us?"

While making these last remarks, the seal held her face close to Dollie's, and her voice was full of pleading. The poor girl did not know what to say. Of course she never had considered the matter in this light. Her recent experience, too, had taught her that those who dwell in the ocean find life as sweet as do those who inhabit the land.

"Please don't blame me," she said finally. "I love seal-skin because it's so warm and nice, but I never thought where it came from, and no one told me. Now, I wouldn't wear it any more for anything, and I'll ask the other girls not to.

Brother Bob won't, either, I'm sure. Can't we talk about something that's pleasant? All this is so horr'ble."

"Let's consider what we're down here for," advised the practical Miss Martha. "Perhaps Miss Seal can tell us where we can find the old King of the Seals. You recollect Mrs. Turtle said he could give us some pointers about the hot spring."

"Why, you must mean my grandfather," replied Miss Seal. "Follow me and I'll take you to him, right straight off."

Gracefully darting ahead, she led her new-found friends on and on until they reached a stony cape that extended far out into the ocean. Here she stopped.

"Now you must come on shore," explained she. "The King is resting on his throne of rocks, and will talk to you there."

"Not I," shouted Sir Owl. "Not I. You may announce to the King that Sir Oliver Owl, the wisest being in all the universe, here awaits him. Let him visit me. It is not becoming that I should go to him."

"Nor can I land here, either," added the Lieutenant. "See, the ground is covered in all directions with rolling, tossing animals of huge size. If one of them should fall on me, I'd be mashed flat as a pancake."

"Then you and I must try it alone, Miss Martha," said Dollie. "Lottie can't leave the water, and no one ever knows what Ann wants to do. Who's 'fraid? Seals aren't any more than big cats."

"Big cats," echoed Sir Owl. "That's it exactly. And what is more to be shunned? Remember how Ann tried to trick the Lieutenant on the boat? What faith can you have in this Miss Seal?"

"Sir Owl's right," chimed in Lottie. "Had a grandmother once. She was smarter than everything. Taught me to look out for sea creatures that wear fur. 'Skin and scales,' said she, 'show good breeding. Hair means bad blood.' She knew what she was talking 'bout, too."

"I-just-don't-care," answered Dollie, sticking out her dimpled chin defiantly. "We're going anyway. Didn't that merman tell us to find the

hot water in the bottom of the ocean? And
didn't we get into a dreadful muss 'cause we
forgot what he said and tried that boat? Now,
I say we'll have lots more trouble if we don't
talk to King Seal, like Mrs. Turtle wanted us
to."

Bidding them wait for her where they were,
she grasped Miss Martha in her arms, and
walked up on the shore.

From the start the journey promised to be a
hard one, for the entire cape was carpeted with
seals of all sizes, and in all possible positions.
Some were snarling, some were smiling, and
some were calling one to the other. Apparently
there was not room anywhere for one more, and
yet others were arriving constantly.

However, Miss Seal knew the way. She directed her companions to follow with her a tiny
path that wound inland through the almost solid
mass of wriggling creatures. They did as requested, but with reluctance which changed to
fear as the beasts closed in behind them and entirely cut off their retreat. Nor was this fear lessened
when one great furry fellow, raising himself on

his tail and flippers, roared out: "Who are these two intruders? Who are they?"

Promptly another giant, from the opposite side of the point, bellowed back in a voice of thunder, "A girl and her friend! That's who they are!"

"And what do they seek here? What do they seek here?"

"A seal-skin muff and a seal-skin cap. That's what they seek!"

Then together they shouted to the assembled herd, "What shall we do with them? What shall we do with them?"

In reply, all the hundreds and hundreds of seals pointed their noses in the air and bawled in chorus:

"There is plenty of seal-skin here! Let us keep them until they find a muff and a cap! Let us keep them! Ho! ho! Ho! ho!"

At this threat Dollie's heart almost stopped beating. After all, had she done right to venture ashore?

CHAPTER XI

TO THE SOUTH HOLE

CHAPTER XI

TO THE SOUTH HOLE

At length the three, carefully picking their path, reached a high, flat-topped stone that answered for a throne. On its crest reclined a portly seal, whose wrinkled face and gray whiskers attested his great age. At the sight of the visitors, he uttered a piercing cry. Instantly the entire Point became perfectly quiet, save for the distant mumbling of the surf.

"What strangers have you here?" he inquired, sternly.

"A little girl, Dollie Lane, and her friend, Miss Martha," answered Miss Seal. "They want to ask you some questions. Please, sir, be good to them."

"Yes, your honor," said Dollie, "we've come ever and ever so far to have a chat with you." As she never before had addressed a real king, she was not sure that "your honor" was the correct expression, but it sounded all right.

183

"Please, isn't there a hot spring down here somewhere? Mrs. Turtle thought you could tell us."

"Mrs. Turtle is a silly gossip," replied the king, sharply. "Unbidden you have come into the kingdom which belongs to us and to those over whom we reign. Men and the children of men always have been our enemies. To you and to your friend we shall make known none of our secrets. It but remains for us to decide upon your fate. What is your pleasure, oh my subjects?" he called forth, in clear tones.

Again arose the chorus, "Keep the girl and her friend until they find the muff and the cap! Ho, ho! Ho, ho!"

"We must be guided by the wishes of our people," said the old king, finally. "Bother us no longer; we would meditate;" and his head sunk upon his breast, as though in sleep.

It seemed no use to argue with him, so Dollie and Miss Martha commenced to hunt for a nook where they could plan what to do next. Finally they discovered a bare spot on which Dollie seated herself and drew Miss Martha close to her breast. As Miss Seal had vanished, no other friend was there to comfort her, and she and Miss Martha began to wonder if they had not been led into a trap even as Sir Owl declared the Lieutenant had been beguiled onto the boat.

Serious indeed was their plight. They stubbornly had put themselves beyond the protection of their companions. Scarcely could they hope, unobserved, to escape to the sea, and if they managed to flee inland, they had not the slightest idea where they were, or whether they would be able to find the way home. Three courses were open to them. They could calmly await their fate; they could make a dash for the ocean; or they could try the land; which should it be?

While thus they were deliberating, Dollie chanced to stretch forth one of her hands along the ground. With an exclamation of fright, she drew it back quickly.

"Mercy me," she screamed, "I've poked up a whole bunch of snakes!"

"Guess again," chuckled the voice of Lieutenant Lobster, placing a huge claw in her lap, so that she might be sure it really was he. "I couldn't stay away any longer, so I managed to work myself up here without being squashed, although I had many narrow escapes. Now, while I may not be able to help you, I at least can share your doom."

Dollie's only answer was to stroke his back lovingly.

"You ought to have been with me just now," he chatted, as he realized the necessity of keeping in good spirits. "Every once in a while, with my claws, I'd nip some seal's fat side. He'd accuse his neighbor of biting him. There are dozens of 'em quarreling all along the line, and there'll be some jolly scraps in the morning. We'll have lots of fun if we're around to watch them. Well, if here isn't Ann! Whatever do you suppose she's been up to?"

"I've been fighting," answered she, and her ruffled hair and swelling tail bore out her words. "What's a seal but a big rat, anyway? My, but I wish I had my stiff, sharp claws back! Then I'd make the fur fly, I tell you. But these brutes make more noise than I can, and they're so damp my clammy paws don't bother 'em the way they did the cook; but I've had some exercise, anyway."

"'Twould tickle you to see Sir Oliver," she rattled on. "He's all swelled up with pride and is rehearsing a grand speech he's going to make when the King of the Seals calls on him. And Lottie, too! He's simply wild because he can't leave the water. Poor wee chap! He can't do much because he's so tiny. Told me the other day he wished he were big like a whale. Thinks about this most all the time, and sings a queer little verse that wise grandmother of his taught him. It runs like this:

> "'If we are wee,
>   We'd rather be
> Not wee. For size we sigh;
>   But since we're wee,
>   'Tis plain that we
> Wee must be till we die.'"

"What an odd song!" exclaimed Dollie. The nonsense of the Lieutenant and Ann had put both her and Miss Martha in good humor. "We, wee, w-e-e-e; why, it sounds like the squeal of a little pink piggie caught in a fence."

While all were laughing at this remark, they

were surprised to hear, close by, the voice of Miss Seal. "Lie down, all of you," she whispered. "Let me tell you something quick while the mob is dozing.

"You can't get through by fighting. These great beasts simply would roll all over you. It's useless, too, for you to plan to steal away along the path we followed after we landed; but there's another walk which leads from here to a cliff overhanging the sea. Once there, you could drop into the water safely, as it's now high tide. Let's try. Dollie, lie down and creep behind me. If you're detected after a while, jump up, run straight forward, and when you reach the edge, leap off. Hurry, now, and remember!"

Dollie was more than willing to make the attempt. Grasping Miss Martha carefully, she crawled slowly after Miss Seal. To the hem of her skirt clung Lieutenant Lobster, that he might not lose the way and also that he might be helped over the rougher places. Ann, of course, could return without aid.

Cautiously they filed along. Now and then

they stopped to breathe, or because the track was blocked; but without other difficulty they progressed until nearly the whole distance had been passed.

Then came peril. It chanced that an old and wise seal, with an acute sense of smell, was lying close to the trail. Miss Seal passed him without trouble, but with Dollie he suspected something wrong. Then her dress came in contact with his nose. That was enough. Instantly, by means of a loud cry, he gave the alarm and grasped her frock firmly between his teeth. Disaster was near at hand.

This was the time for her to show her courage. Springing to her feet, she struck the seal such a resounding whack with her dagger that he released his clutch and lay limp upon the ground. Then commenced a mad race for the cliff and safety, while the Lieutenant hung on desperately and shouted commands of encouragement. The route was alive with ugly beasts; but luckily the distance was short. Nimbly she stepped on backs, heads, tails and flippers, and, without stumble or mishap, but somewhat out of breath, she reached the goal and jumped into the ocean. How good the water felt! and how glad were she and Miss Martha to be free from their sullen enemies!

Ann, purring her satisfaction, took her place beside them; and Lottie and Sir Oliver, hearing the splash, came rushing up to see what was the matter. At the close of Dollie's explanation, another splash occurred and Miss Seal was seen moving swiftly towards them.

"Oh! I'm so very, very glad you escaped," she cried, as she drew near. "I wouldn't have had you hurt for anything in the world. Whatever made my grandfather so cross, I don't know. It isn't like him at all."

"Perhaps his supper didn't agree with him," suggested Dollie, seriously. "Once my gran'pa John ate pickles and pie just before he went to bed, and he was so cross for a whole week that I couldn't tease one bit of candy from him."

"The cause makes no difference now," re-marked Miss Martha, in her matter-of-fact way. "We're loose again. That's what counts. And if we're ever going to get through and go home,

we better start south again right off. There's
where the hot spring is. If we keep together
and mind our own business, we're bound to
come across it."

"So you want to see the hot spring, do you?"
asked Miss Seal. "Dare I tell you about it? I
guess I will, so you'll know I mean you good
instead of harm. Listen; the hot spring is exactly below the South Hole."

"The South Hole," repeated Miss Martha.
"There's nothing about that in any geography
I ever saw. You must mean the South Pole."

"Not at all," insisted Miss Seal. "You may
have a pole up north, but down here there isn't
any. Perhaps there was long ago, but it's been
pulled out, and has left the loveliest hole in the
world. It beats a merry-go-round, a shoot-the-
chutes, a Ferris wheel, a whirligig and a roller-
coaster, all made into one. You can't miss the
way. Have Lottie steer ahead till he comes to
a place where you have to go north. Then, there
you are!"

"But I'm so 'fraid we'll miss it," cried Dollie.
"If it's a little one, like you set a flag pole in,

we might go right by and never see it at all."

"Trust to me for that," Sir Oliver assured her. "As usual, you can rely on my wisdom. In selecting a house, I always choose a hollow tree with a good south hole. Then the sunlight and the warm breeze keep the nest dry and healthful. Leave it to me to point out to you any south hole we may pass by."

"Yes, you'll know it all right," laughed Miss Seal. "No doubt about that. But will your friends know you, after it's all over? That's what I wonder. Now I must hurry back before I am missed. Good-bye, and good luck!"

"What in the name of common sense makes all these sea creatures dash off before one is half through talking to them?" complained Miss Martha. "I declare, the merman is the only one who has good manners. Mr. Whale, Mrs. Turtle, and now Miss Seal, do not know what it is to be polite."

"Miss Seal is well aware of my wisdom," spoke Sir Owl, "and she feared to have me question her. There's another plot here to drag us into peril. Mark well my words. Twice has

WITHOUT A SINGLE DESERTER, THE ADVENTUROUS BAND SET FORTH

there been trouble because you would not heed me."

"Sir Owl is right," insisted Lottie. "Don't do anything that furry seal tells you to. 'Member what my grandmother said? Grandmother knew everything."

"It is no time to hesitate," cried Lieutenant Lobster, boldly. "Miss Seal but confirms what the others have stated. Whoever may fight against us, surely I and my army shall be victorious. If there be a coward in the ranks, let him fall out. Forward, march!"

These brave words from their commander gave fresh courage to all, and, without one single deserter, the adventurous band set forth. Though little was said, all were excited. Through Miss Seal's actions and words had run a mysterious something which set their blood a-tingle. That strange and extraordinary events were in store for them seemed certain, but nothing must deter them from finding the spring and the Magical Man of Mirth.

Gradually the water grew colder and soon in the distance appeared a long line of dazzling

white, which the explorers knew must be the
edge of a field of ice. While gazing at the
beautiful sight, Lottie almost knocked against
a whale who lazily was diving past.

As may be expected, all paused a moment to
converse with the newcomer, but at first he did
not take any interest in what they said. An
account of the whale they had met farther north
roused him not a bit, nor did the story of the
escape from the seals. It was only when Dollie
mentioned where they were going that he actually awoke.

"The South Hole!" he sputtered, as though he
could not believe his ears. "You don't mean
you are aiming for the South Hole!"

"Yes, sir," answered Dollie, stoutly.

"And you're taking your Miss Martha, and a
lobster and a tiny pilot-fish, and Sir Owl, and
the ghost of a cat?"

"Yes, sir," Dollie repeated.

This announcement was too much for the
whale. His fat sides, his flippers, and even his
tail, wiggled with merriment which could not be
concealed.

"Say, fellows," he sang out to his mates, as soon as he could speak, "this kid here and her outfit are going to, and into, and down the South Hole! Isn't that killing?"

Then the whales—and there were dozens of them—opened their mouths wide and sent forth peals of laughter. Every individual stretched his jaws apart so wide that the upper rested on his back and his nose pointed towards his tail. This position did not agree with them, for they began to choke and sneeze and cough. Finally they made a furious rush for a clear space, whence their snorts of glee could be heard long after the travelers had left them far behind.

"I don't see what's so funny," murmured Dollie with a puzzled look. "But let 'em laugh if they want to. Prob'bly they don't know any better."

"Do not pay any attention to them, my dear," remarked Miss Martha. "It is a good plan to ignore some people entirely. And now what have we here? Can it be we are running into a mad house?"

The party were wending their way among the

ice-floes which here were drifting some distance apart. Hanging onto one of these floes by two long tusks which protruded from his upper jaw was an immense beast, with hairy muzzle, whose ugly appearance had caused Miss Martha's exclamation.

"Well, who are you?" asked Ann, arching her back in anger. "You look like a half-drowned, overgrown wharf-rat. Why don't you climb up or drop off? It makes me nervous to see you sticking by your teeth that way."

"Some folks call me a sea-horse," replied the creature, "but I prefer Mr. Walrus as a name. Don't be afraid; I'm not fierce, though I look so unless I shave every day, which is a bother."

With surprising agility he drew his huge, flabby body onto the ice, and flopped down with a grunt of satisfaction. "You're strangers in this neighborhood," said he. "If you don't mind telling, I wonder what you're doing."

"We're on our way to the hot spring near the South Hole," Dollie replied, somewhat doubtfully.

"You don't mean it!" cried Mr. Walrus.

"And Miss Martha, too? Well, well! And the lobster, and Sir Owl, and all? Yes? Oh me, oh my—what fun, what fun!"

His whole frame wobbled with mirth till the ice-cake rocked, and with a mighty splash off he slid, to be seen no more.

"I don't care a bit," again announced Dollie. "They can laugh and laugh long as it does 'em any good. If there's a jest, I'm going to find out what it is. They can't scare me, so there!"

"Hurrah for you!" shouted the Lieutenant. "You're made of the right stuff, and we'll all stay by you. Now, let us halt no more to talk with passers-by until the Hole has been reached and we have boiled the broth in the hot spring."

But news of the wanderers and their strange mission must have preceded them, for they were not to avoid further teasing. A fat, white bear, taking a sail on a mighty iceberg, spied them down below, and at once became convulsed with hilarity. In a voice that echoed from crag to berg, and echoed back from berg to crag, he roared: "There they are! Look at 'em! Look at 'em, quick! They're bound for the South

Hole. What a joke!" and, like the walrus, he toppled into the ocean. Across the weary wastes of ice and snow came, too, the long-drawn-out howls of the wolves, as they cried one to another: "To the Hole; to the H-o-l-e! oh, o-o-o-oh!"

Yet, true to the decision, there was no pause. Lottie's slim form continually clove the sea; behind him sped the now experienced voyagers. As the Lieutenant proclaimed, the South Hole and the hot spring were to be discovered soon; if they did not want to be, they must move away in a hurry.

"He's right," whispered Dollie to Miss Martha. "We'll get what we want if it takes forever and ever. And after we've found 'em, and fixed the Magical Man of Mirth, and seen the City of Mirth all happy again, we'll go back home. This is lots of fun, but we've been gone a long while and I'm 'fraid papa and mamma are wond'ring where I am."

CHAPTER XII

DOWN THE SOUTH HOLE

CHAPTER XII

DOWN THE SOUTH HOLE

"Oooooo-o-o—o," howled the wolves in the distance.

"To-who-ooo-o-o—o," answered Sir Owl.

"Ever since the first wolf was made," he explained, "he has been trying to toot like an owl; but his efforts are in vain. To produce the sound correctly requires a beak instead of a muzzle, a throat of peculiar shape, and ears like mine, nicely built to detect the slightest discord. Still it is to the credit of those beasts that they endeavor to imitate me. I am the best howler as well as the wisest animal in the world."

So much Dollie heard distinctly, but when the bird continued to boast, in low tones, his words were drowned in a gradual din which for some time had been increasing in volume. It seemed as though the tooting and the howling had merged into a moaning, and the moaning into a strange humming, like that given forth by a circular saw when whirling in rapid motion.

"Whatever is making such a racket," shouted Dollie. "It 'minds me of a peg-top, but it must be a mighty big one. And where could it be spinning? Nonsense; it isn't a top, but what is it?"

"Let me give you the desired information," answered Sir Owl, at the top of his voice. "Some day you may learn to reason things out for yourself. What made the South Hole? The pulling up of the South Pole. And what is done with poles when they are pulled up? They are sawed into planks. Someone near is sawing the South Pole. That's what makes the noise."

"Well, did you ever?" shrieked Miss Martha. "That bird will be the death of me yet. Who ever heard of a saw-mill way out in the ocean? And who wants planks in a place like this? Do you suppose someone is making a cradle for a baby whale, or a roost for you when you are sleepy?"

This discussion, however, was cut short because it was too hard work to talk in such a tumult. Then the sudden appearance of other animals demanded attention. Here, two whales churned the water like boats in a spirited race for a prize. There, a seal, outstripping everybody else, slipped ahead like a brown streak.

Not far away, a clumsy white bear puffed and blew in a violent effort to keep up with the procession. Evidently something of great interest to many lay not far beyond, but what it was the visitors could not ascertain. Now and then they hailed one of their strange companions, but received no reply. Every particle of breath seemed to be needed for other purposes.

The next change was in the action of the ocean. Although still proceeding directly south, Lottie and his comrades at the same time were being carried towards the east by a cross-current which grew stronger and stronger as they advanced. He could offset this side motion only by heading somewhat to the west, as one who rows across a rapid river points the bow of his boat above the place where he really hopes to land.

In this way, all went well for a time. Then the rush of the water grew so powerful that practically no headway was made. The only progress was with the swift flood, wherever it might be tending, and the only encouragement lay in the fact that the whale and the other travelers also had ceased struggling, and, with their noses to the south, were drifting quietly.

What was happening? It was Miss Martha who made the discovery. "We're sailing in a ring," cried she. "Don't you remember, a while ago that big white star near the horizon was in front of us? Now she's straight behind. Watch, and soon she'll be in front again."

Her words proved true; and moreover, the circles kept growing smaller and smaller. This could be detected because the star appeared to change her position so frequently. Round and round they were steadily rushing, and nearer and nearer to the central point they were constantly being drawn. What was the explanation, and what would be the result?

"I know what's the matter," exclaimed Dollie, with a note of alarm in her voice. "We're caught in a terrible whirlpool! It's made by the ocean pouring into the South Hole, and that causes the noise. Oh, Miss Martha! we'll spin and spin, faster and faster, till we reach the middle, and then we'll be sucked down where perhaps we'll never come up!"

Miss Martha, by her answer, showed her grit. "Don't get scared, girlie," said she. "These whales and things wouldn't swim right into the hole if it's going to hurt 'em. We can stand it as long as they can."

"Of course we can," added the Lieutenant earnestly. "You mustn't be alarmed, my child. Bravery is half the battle. If the hot spring is at the bottom of this howling hole, down the howling hole we must go."

By these remarks Dollie was somewhat reassured. Anyway, she decided to take things calmly and not to give up until the last moment. Notwithstanding this resolve, her nerve almost left her a little later, when for one entire revolution they remained on the rim of what looked like a gigantic funnel.

They could gaze straight down into the whirling pit, which grew narrower and narrower, until the base seemed to be simply a foam-covered dot. At several points on the sides could be descried portions of various animals thrust out into the air as they twisted about in their descent. Truly, the South Hole had been found.

"I shall go no farther," shouted Sir Owl. "This whole affair promises to be one of disgrace to a bird of my dignity. I shall not have one single tail feather left and my fine voice will be ruined. Stop it, stop it, I say!"

As well might he have tried to hinder the rising of the sun. With an unearthly yowl from Ann, over the edge they swept; lower and lower they dropped; dizzily and more dizzily they swung; less and less in size became the circles. To Dollie, the very air and water seemed filled with feathers, claws, ghostly paws, tails, and straying locks of her own hair.

So, into the very point they plunged. Intense darkness surrounded them. The roar of the water prevented speech and its churning and turmoil took away their breath. Now came the supreme test. From where they were, they never could regain the surface. Would they manage to swim off, or would they remain to toss for ever and ever? These were anxious questions.

For some moments it seemed certain that the suction was holding them. What would be the end? A quick pressure from the Lieutenant's claw first called Dollie's attention to a possible change. Was it for the better?

Yes; she was standing upright, and she could feel that her heels were making bigger loops than her head. This showed that she was sinking, and that the whirlpool below now changed from smaller to larger rings, like an inverted funnel. Perhaps together the two funnels made a huge hour-glass, with Dollie and her friends exactly in the neck between the globes.

This proved to be the case. Down they continued to go, and, as they went, the rings expanded and enclosed a space filled with pure air. The current, too, became more and more gentle. With a final spin, they softly touched the bed of the ocean, which, to their joy, consisted of fine, golden sand.

"Well, well!" chuckled the Lieutenant as he reached the ground. "Wasn't that a twister? For once in my life I believe I've had enough of

the water. I'm almost ready to turn land-crab.
Let's go outside, dry off and straighten ourselves
out. My claws, feelers, legs and tail are all in
a snarl. My! aren't they bright and clean?"

"But look at me! What do you think of
me?" shrieked Sir Owl, beside himself with
wrath. "Behold my feathers. In a thousand
ways they are crossed and twisted. I feel like
a picked chicken. Some one shall suffer for this
outrage!"

No one made reply, because words would only
increase his anger; and all, excepting Lottie, who
could not live in the air, followed the Lieutenant out into the round park. Last came Sir Oliver, now grumbling softly to himself as he tried
to smooth his rumpled plumage.

"Well, how did you like it?" asked a deep
bass voice, almost before the little party were
fairly settled.

Looking around, they saw a jolly white bear
sitting on his haunches near by. His eyes
twinkled roguishly, and his red tongue hung
from his mouth, as though he were tired.

"Very much indeed," answered Dollie politely;

"but we might have had more fun if we'd been sure all the time that we'd land in a spot like this."

"That's the point exactly," chuckled the bear, "and that's why we laughed and wouldn't tell you. Every one's frightened the first trip. I'm the bear that fell from the berg. I followed on purpose to watch you and enjoy the sport."

"But isn't the result fine?" he continued. "Beats a shave, haircut and shampoo. Look at my coat; dustless as if it'd been run through a carpet-cleaner. Some one'll be taking me for a woolly lamb if I'm not careful. See that whale, too; skin slick and clean as if he'd just had a massage. Same with the seal. His coat hasn't a speck of dirt on it; couldn't be in better condition if he'd just visited a furrier. Everyone ought to come here once a month regularly. You will, if you get the habit started."

"I don't know but that I'd be glad to," agreed Dollie, though somewhat doubtfully, "but we didn't do it for the fun of the thing. We're looking for a hot spring, and now I don't b'lieve it's here at all. Isn't that mean?"

"A hot spring," said the bear. "Why, it's right under me. I'm lying on it to cure a bruise on my side where I bumped myself when I fell. Look, here it is."

The bear arose, and all gathered around the place whereon he had lain. To their great joy, the sand, for a space as big around as a dinner-plate, was tossing and seething, and in the center of the mass was a spot of clear water, merrily bubbling and boiling. To remove the slightest doubt, Dollie stuck one of her fingers into the hole.

"Ouch!" she exclaimed, as she quickly withdrew it and thrust it into her mouth. "That's hotter than a stove. Now don't anybody bother me or say a word. I'm going to cook."

Up as far as her elbows, she turned the sleeves of her waist, just as she had seen her mother do when working in the kitchen, and from her pocket she took the shell with its precious contents. Then she deftly withdrew the clay and the pebble, and carefully pushed the shell itself into the sand close to the scalding water.

As the heat penetrated the brass covering, the stuff in the shell began to simmer and then to boil, while above it hovered a tiny cloud of black vapor. A few moments later, Dollie, with a self-satisfied air, wrapped her right hand in her handkerchief so that she would not be burned, cautiously removed the shell, again corked it securely by means of the pebble and clay, and cooled it by sticking it into the ocean. Then she put it back into her pocket.

"There," she cried joyously, "now that's done. Don't you think I am a beaut'ful cook-lady, Miss Martha?"

"You are always sweet and beautiful, my dear child, and one can be a lady in the kitchen as well as in the parlor," she answered. "Now let us hurry and find the Magical Man of Mirth. At last the broth is ready for him, I'm thankful to say."

"But where shall we first look for him?" questioned the Lieutenant. "I have been thinking it over, and it seems to me, however dangerous and disagreeable it may be, we must go back to the depths of the ocean and search the caves and caverns. There it was we came across the devil-fish, and there shall we discover this magical villain. Where would he be so apt to lurk as with hideous monsters, just as was said by the soothsayer in the City of Mirth?"

The plan of the Lieutenant seemed a sensible one, and all began to prepare for the return journey.

"If you wish to go back easily," said the bear, "I'll tell you how. All the water that falls down the South Hole has to leave in a hurry to make room for more. It's formed a stream that, close to the ground, rushes north as straight as an arrow. You don't have to do any work yourself, and you're whisked along faster than you could swim. The entrance is in that dark place back there."

Everybody agreed that the bear's plan was an excellent one. So with a good-bye and a hearty expression of thanks, and with a final glance at the twirling dome above, they plunged into the sea at the point indicated. Immediately, without the slightest effort on their part, they were carried away with great rapidity.

This seemed to suit Sir Oliver, who by this time had fully recovered from his indignation. To show his relief, he straightened up in front of his companions and, with many a stately bow and gesture, recited the following lines, which he declared he had composed for that especial occasion:

"The express that departs at 2:02
Always starts with a hoot and a toot, too;
And so, far away,
We six ride to-day
In a car built for only two, too."

Miss Martha immediately cried out that the car was big enough for a dozen; Dollie was certain that she had not heard a single hoot nor toot; and Lottie thought it must be at least 4.04 instead of 2.02.

"Listen and learn," cried Ann, for once coming to the assistance of the owl. "You show that you know nothing about poetry. Now, I've dreamed poetry day after day, and meowed it night after night. To make a verse, you place, one below the other, a column of words which rhyme; in lines before them you insert a few more words, so that all taken together jingle.

This completes the poem. Then you search for a meaning if there be one, and you invent a meaning if there be none. In Sir Oliver's case——"

"No lecture for me," interrupted Miss Martha. "I'm going to take it easy." Dollie's blinking eyes clearly showed how she felt in the matter. Lottie had poised himself with motionless tail and fins. Lieutenant Lobster and Sir Owl no longer were paying attention to what was going on. So Ann cut short her remarks and curled herself up in a ball.

Thus, snug and cozy, they swiftly drifted by rocks and boulders, around table-lands and mountains, and at times through beds of queerly shaped sea-plants, but ever onward and onward. No one kept any track of the distance. When the proper place was reached, they intended to leave the current, and to commence the search for the Magical Man of Mirth, with whom they might be compelled to fight, even as they had battled to release the mermaid from the wicked serpent.

Lucky it is that they had the chance to rest

and to recover their strength, for, great as had been the dangers which had attended the task already accomplished, the gravest peril of all, as you shall see, was still in store for them.

CHAPTER XIII

THE TASK COMPLETED

CHAPTER XIII

THE TASK COMPLETED

Riding on a train always makes one drowsy, and likewise this journey caused these travelers to feel sleepy. Dollie gave in first; then Miss Martha; and the Lieutenant was beginning to nod his head, when suddenly all were aroused by a scream from Lottie and by a stern command, "Hold up your hands; quick, now!"

"Robbers! Train robbers!" cried Lottie; and, though thoroughly frightened, Dollie scarcely could refrain from smiling when he kept on muttering to himself: "Course there's more trouble; I knew it. Comes from 'sociating with that furry seal. Needn't tell me my grandmother didn't know what she was talking 'bout." But, while listening to Lottie, she had obeyed the order of the bandits. Not so the Lieutenant, who, as an old soldier, was ashamed at being caught napping.

"Up with your hands, there, Lobster!" came

the second command. "If you don't, we'll bite off your head."

"I have no hands," growled the Lieutenant.

"Your claws, then! No time for fooling!"

Above his head went Lieutenant Lobster's claws. What else could he do? In front of him and his charges were two large, fierce fishes. Two others guarded the rear. All four appeared to be principally mouth and teeth. The front view was much as though one were gazing into an open keg, driven full of long, sharp spikes. If those jaws once closed over the Lieutenant or any portion of the body of one of his companions, the result would be disastrous.

"What can I do?" wailed Ann, as though in great distress. "I haven't any hands or claws. Please, sirs, shall I lie on my back and wriggle my paws, or arch my back and stick up my tail?"

"No talking," was the sharp response.

"What must I do?" whimpered Lottie, who beyond doubt was greatly frightened. "Haven't any hands, paws or claws. Want me to stand on my head and wave *my* tail, too?"

"And what do you desire concerning me?" asked Sir Owl solemnly. "You observe I have no hands nor paws. My tail, too, is almost entirely gone, through circumstances I now have not time to relate. With all my wisdom, I do not know what to do for you, unless I flap my wings and toot, or stand on my head and kick my legs."

"Silence, all of you," cried one of the robbers, as Miss Martha began to speak. "Where's that cat?"

To the astonishment of her captors, Ann was not to be seen. She had vanished before their very eyes.

"Now, to one side with you," was the next instruction; "and if any more of you bolt, you'll feel our teeth."

As they stood on the sand, without the current, the Lieutenant managed to find his tongue.

"What do you mean by this outrage?" demanded he. "You must be crazy."

"Not at all," said the leader, he who had the biggest mouth and the sharpest teeth. "We are scouts detailed to find delicacies to grace the

table of our beloved master, King Bitemintwo I.
Yesterday he succeeded to the throne of King
Eatemalive III, who died suddenly from getting
a shark stuck crosswise in his throat. To-morrow
will be a day of great feasting, in which we in-
vite you to take part."

"Oh, ho! Oh, ho!" laughed the others.
"That's a good one. Take part *in* the feast; be
part *of* the feast. What a joker you are!"

Then the four whispered together, and Dollie
could catch expressions such as these: "Bring on
the little fish first;" "And the big bird for the
second course;" "Then Dollie for the red meat;"
"The lobster next; salad a la Lieutenant, we'll
call it;" "We can crack Miss Slate into pieces
and serve her with the nuts;" "Won't the king
be tickled when he sees what we've caught?"

The thought that she and her friends were to
serve as food for the banquet of King Bitemintwo I was not particularly pleasing to Dollie,
yet escape seemed impossible, because the first
four brigands had been joined by four more,
equally fierce. One of these swam above the
prisoners, one below, and one on each side. Thus,

with two ahead and two bringing up the rear, they were surrounded entirely.

As she tried to think of some way out of their unwelcome position, a fresh and still greater peril threatened. This was heralded by the sudden return of Ann, with terror written in every line of her ghostly face. Her fear was none the less real because for her friends and not for herself.

"Away! Away! For your lives! For your lives!!" she shrieked. "The deadliest demon of all the deep is pursuing!"

One glance proved the truth of her warning. The devil-fish, the seals, the serpent, even the robbers, seemed as puny as new-born kittens in comparison with the monster who was following her. His thick-scaled body, long as a telephone pole and thrice as big, was furnished with sets of fins, large as an eagle's wings, while below each fin swayed a short and powerful leg, sharp-clawed like those of an alligator; his jaws ended in a beak, pointed and cruel; his dark red eyes gleamed balefully; while from a hole in the top of his head poured a cloud of foul and darkly colored steam that trailed far behind him, as the smoke from a locomotive.

At the sight of this apparition, a wild fright seized upon captors and captives. Yet, quickly as they dodged, one of the robbers was over-hauled and swallowed whole. Then, after an instant's delay, the fiend swept on in search of other victims.

"He's running a-muck," shouted the Lieutenant. "Our only chance is to outswim him. Do your best. It's life or death!"

Unnecessary warning. Already Ann and Lottie had set off at a terrific pace. Close behind them glided Miss Martha. After her, side by side, struggled Dollie and Sir Oliver, swimming as they never had swum before. Last of all trailed the Lieutenant, in desperation, grimly hanging by his claws to the gown of the one and the remnants of the tail of the other.

Here was shown the real affection which united the members of this faithful band. Ann would not desert Lottie. He, in turn, though the fastest swimmer of all, set a pace no swifter than the others could maintain; and Dollie and

Sir Owl made no complaint, though hampered by the dragging of Lieutenant Lobster's body. The fate of one should be the fate of all.

Despite their most earnest efforts, the beast gained upon them. Yard by yard, foot by foot, inch by inch, closer and closer he crept. Without looking back, they could feel his deadly presence, and in some unknown way, Dollie realized that she would be the first object of his attack. With a groan of despair, she shut her eyes as she heard the grinding of his mighty jaws, and when she actually felt them close and tug upon her skirt, she knew that she was lost.

No, not lost. At least, there was a brief respite, for the dreaded beak did not cut into her. Why was this? Curiosity overcame her fear, so that she glanced over her shoulder. Nothing now was chasing them. At her signal, all stopped and gazed in wonder. The monster indeed had vanished; but in his stead, almost beneath them, on a patch of yellow sand, lay outstretched the body of a little man, clad in a flowing robe of many colors.

A black skull-cap fitted closely over his hairless head, and his coal-black eyes, in strange contrast with the deathly pallor of his face, were fixed on them intently. With a feeble wave of his arm, he beckoned to them to approach. Who was he? Was it possible—could he really be—yes, beyond question, he was—the Magical Man of Mirth!

"'Tis he! 'Tis he!" tooted Sir Owl. "I knew who he was all the time." But such boasting sounded strangely out of place.

"Hush! Do be quiet," urged Dollie, as she seated herself beside the little fellow, and took his head into her lap. "See, he's suffering. I've tried and tried to catch him, and now I'm sorry for him."

"Never mind," said the man. "I am in no pain, but my end is near. How I have been changed back from the strange shape I had taken, I know not, but in some way I have swallowed the mystic broth, which only the Sorceress of the City of Mirth knows how to prepare."

"I can tell you," remarked Miss Martha. "We fixed the broth the way she told us to and put it in a shell in Dollie's pocket. When you bit at her and caught her dress, you tore out the pocket and gulped it down, shell and all."

"It is well," answered the man. "The saying runs in our family that they who live by magic shall perish by magic. The Queen did wrong when she discharged me, but a greater wrong was mine when I cast over her and over her city the spell of sorrow. Let me right this while I may."

Raising his frail hands, he waved them thrice to the north, thrice to the south, thrice to the west and thrice to the east; then, in faint tones he murmured:

"A spell have I cast o'er the City of Mirth
Through a power bestowed upon me at my birth;
But now, as I flit to a far-away shore,
Let the Queen and her city be happy once more."

After so speaking, he began to disappear. First his right ear vanished completely; next, his left leg; then his right arm; and thus piece by piece he passed away before Dollie's astonished eyes, until nothing remained on the golden sand but the shell of polished brass, now empty, but still with never a crack.

"Oh, dear," sighed Dollie, with a little sob;

"I b'lieve he was a real nice man after all, and I do hope he's happy, wherever he's gone. Don't you, Miss Martha? And do you s'pose the Queen of the City of Mirth is laughing again, and the cloud is all white and dry?"

"I certainly do," answered Miss Martha, "and it's high time we started back. First we must visit the cloud and pay our respects to the Queen. Then I'm going to take you straight home and put you to bed."

"Miss Martha speaks the truth," agreed the Lieutenant. "You have served faithfully under my leadership. Since our task has been accomplished, the army must disband. Let our goodbyes be brief, though none the less sincere. We old soldiers have learned to conceal our feelings. Dollie, point the way to the surface. Forward, march!"

Silently they rose to the lighter and warmer regions, and, all too soon for Dollie, again they floated just beneath the rolling waves.

"The cloud is right above us," announced Sir Owl, after poking his head into the air, "and it is white as it ever was. It gratifies me greatly to behold what I have done. Now I must go and receive my reward from the Queen. The whole heavens shall ring with applause for my brave acts."

Dollie was too much overcome at the thought of parting from her three good friends, to notice these grand words. Time after time she shook Lieutenant Lobster's claw, patted Ann's ghost of a back and smoothed Lottie's glittering side. Then, while Miss Martha spoke her adieus with stately grace, as became a lady of her years, the child climbed onto Sir Owl's back and placed Miss Martha in her lap. The owl's farewell consisted of one single toot; and once more upward they sped.

Farther and farther below them dropped the billowy ocean. Nearer and nearer approached the fair, white cloud. Soon Dollie could hear strains of soft, sweet music, mingled with shouts of happiness and laughter as though from children at play. In response to Sir Owl's toots of victory, a crowd of little people, clad in pink and white and gold, appeared at one of the portals, and as he safely landed before them, they commenced to carol a hymn of greeting.

The warder, too, was there, but no longer bowed and weary. Instead, he was dancing up and down like a school-boy on Saturday morning.

"Welcome! thrice welcome!" he cried, in joyous tones. "The Queen awaits you in her throne-room. Let us lead you thither."

The little people, still singing sweetly, formed in two long lines and with the warder in the lead and Dollie, Miss Martha and Sir Oliver bringing up the rear, the march commenced.

What a contrast from the previous visit! Then, everywhere had been darkness, dampness and sorrow. Now the pathway beneath was white and dry as polished marble; above and on each side, the surface softly gleamed and sparkled like banks of snow on a moonlight night. The balmy air was filled with music from some hidden source. Best of all, the faces of everyone who could be seen, and the voices of everyone who could be heard, showed the presence of perfect peace without one trace of pain.

When the procession entered the Queen's room, she stepped down from her throne, and extended

both her hands to Dollie, in greeting. Very
beautiful was she with her laughing eyes and
dimpled cheeks, while myriads of pure white diamonds shone in her dark hair, and twinkled like
dewdrops along her gown of gold.

"I cannot tell you in words how much I thank
you," said the Queen to Dollie, "and Miss Martha, too, for I know she helped you; nor must I
forget Sir Owl, who carried you. I know, also,
that you did all this for me through love and
not for pay. Still it would please me to give
you something as a token of my favor. What
do you most desire?"

"Eleven fat field-mice," spoke up Sir Owl,
grandly, "and seven plump little rabbits."
Though the question had been addressed to Dollie, he could not imagine that praise could be
meant for anyone but him.

"Very well," said the Queen, with a smile.
"You shall have them immediately. And Dollie?"

"I don't know of anything in the world I
want right now, 'cept to see my mamma," answered the girl.

"And it is a very sweet desire," replied the Queen, "but before you go home, I hope you will accept, as a gift from me, this stone—the famous Enoh-pelet stone—the most precious in all my collection. You will notice the name is engraved upon one of its sides."

In Dollie's hands she placed a small cube, hard, smooth, dark green and with a hole clear through its center.

"How pretty," cried the child, "but what is it for?"

"Hush!" whispered Miss Martha. "It isn't polite to ask questions about a gift. Use your senses."

Dollie touched the stone with her tongue; it was tasteless. She peeped into the hole, but found nothing. She held it before her nose; there was no odor. Then she chanced to spell the name from right to left, telep-hone. With an exclamation of surprise, she pressed the tiny hole against her ear.

"Dollie, Dollie, where are you?" she heard her mother calling. "It's time for you to come in and go to bed."

"I HOPE YOU WILL ACCEPT THIS STONE—THE FAMOUS ENOH-PELET STONE"

"I'm coming, mamma, I'm coming," she answered, without thinking where she was.

Swish! Cloud and fairies had vanished. Swish! she was falling, falling, falling. Swish! and she opened her eyes to find herself sitting again in the swing beneath the old oak-tree in the glorious backyard at home. In her lap lay Miss Martha, safe and sound, while a rustling in the branches overhead probably was being caused by the wings of Sir Oliver Owl.

"Dollie, Dollie, where are you?" she heard her mother calling. "It's time for you to come in and go to bed."

"I'm coming, mamma, I'm coming," she answered, and off she scampered.

It is great fun to wander far and wide, but, when mother calls, home is the best place after all.